"If I agree, how long do you expect Leo and me to stay in Ghana for?"

"The first few years of his life at the very least. More if we decide that Leo would be better off by us remaining a unit rather than apart."

Astonishment had her gaping for several seconds before she collected herself. "Excuse me? Did you say the first few *years*? I'm not sure what sorts of guests you invite to your home to visit, but I don't intend to be one of them. And most definitely not for that length of time."

Ekow's intense eyes rested mockingly on her, and Eva was sure a snort left his throat before he strolled forward to stand before her. "You misunderstand, my dear. You're not coming to Accra as my guest. You and our son are coming to live with me. *Permanently*. He's going to take my name and his place as my rightful heir. And you, Evangeline, are going to live under my roof as my wife."

Ghana's Most Eligible Billionaires

Power, scandal and forbidden lovers!

The infamous Quayson brothers, Atu and Ekow, seem to have it all, but the power that comes with their gargantuan name holds more weight than they bargained for... The higher you are to the top, the harder the fall. And with all that power, love is the last thing on their minds—until two enigmatic women show them that surrendering to passion may be worth the ultimate risk...

Read Atu and Amelie's story in
Bound by Her Rival's Baby

Discover Ekow and Evangeline's story in
A Vow to Claim His Hidden Son

Both available now!

Maya Blake

—

A VOW TO CLAIM HIS HIDDEN SON

HARLEQUIN

PRESENTS

Recycling programs for this product may not exist in your area.

ISBN-13: 978-1-335-56866-3

A Vow to Claim His Hidden Son

Copyright © 2022 by Maya Blake

This is a work of fiction. Names, characters, places and incidents are either the product of the author's imagination or are used fictitiously. Any resemblance to actual persons, living or dead, businesses, companies, events or locales is entirely coincidental.

For questions and comments about the quality of this book, please contact us at CustomerService@Harlequin.com.

Harlequin Enterprises ULC
22 Adelaide St. West, 41st Floor
Toronto, Ontario M5H 4E3, Canada
www.Harlequin.com

Printed in U.S.A.

Maya Blake's hopes of becoming a writer were born when she picked up her first romance at thirteen. Little did she know, her dream would come true! Does she still pinch herself every now and then to make sure it's not a dream? Yes, she does! Feel free to pinch her, too, via Twitter, Facebook or Goodreads! Happy reading!

Books by Maya Blake

Harlequin Presents

The Sicilian's Banished Bride
The Commanding Italian's Challenge
The Greek's Hidden Vows
Reclaimed for His Royal Bed

Passion in Paradise

Kidnapped for His Royal Heir

The Notorious Greek Billionaires

Claiming My Hidden Son
Bound by My Scandalous Pregnancy

Ghana's Most Eligible Billionaires

Bound by Her Rival's Baby

Visit the Author Profile page
at Harlequin.com for more titles.

To Mansa, my gorgeous baby sis.
This one is for you!

PROLOGUE

SOMEONE WAS HACKING his bank.

Again.

If Ekow Quayson hadn't been so infuriated at the ease with which the hacker had infiltrated his formidable internet firewall, he would've been impressed. But his sense of humour had left the building after the third breach.

'How the hell is this still happening?' he barked into the phone. 'Correct me if I'm wrong, but don't I pay you astronomical sums to ensure this sort of thing doesn't happen?'

He didn't need to be in the same room to know that his cyber security team were shaking in their boots. He hadn't yet taken the final step of firing them after weeks…no, *months*…of the cat-and-mouse game this hacker was playing with him only because they were the best—*supposedly*—on the market.

'Sir, they're using a very sophisticated system. One we haven't seen before. But we're attempting to—'

'Stop attempting and get it done! You're cyber security experts. It's your job to make sure no system, sophisticated or otherwise, messes with my bank. You're failing. Fix it. Now.'

'Yes, sir. Our counterparts in South Africa are working on the issue right now. That's where we pinpointed the last few attacks. We should… It'll be taken care of within the next few hours.'

Ekow froze in his chair. 'Did you say South Africa?' he asked, choosing to ignore the false confidence his security chief had layered on his response. They were all skating on thin ice, and he wouldn't hesitate to fire them if the breach wasn't sorted this time.

'Yes, sir. We're moments away from tracking the hacker down.'

Ekow barely heard the response as his fingers curled into a fist on his desk and a curious roiling started inside him.

South Africa.

He knew he was giving too much power to a geographical location, but the slow, unrelenting knots tightening in his gut mocked that knowledge.

South Africa… Specifically Cape Town…

The place he'd met *her.*

By his very strict record, he should've forgotten her by now. Moved on to the next available woman as he did every few months. It was the way he preferred things. It ensured mutual enjoyment without inviting notions of permanence. Since he'd turned thirty, two years ago, it was as if he had switched on an unknown beacon to the opposite sex, urging them not to take seriously his 'just fun, nothing heavy' edict when it came to relationships.

Every single one had eventually discovered he'd meant it, of course. Because he'd sworn off entanglements of any sort except the very transient kind. And if those brief liaisons with the opposite sex had only got briefer and less enjoyable in the last few years it was no one's business but his own.

When life had taught you that emotional connections led to disappointment and devastation, you learned the very real lesson that keeping your emotions out of things was the best way forward.

He'd learned that truth up close.

First by observing his father's patently biased relationship with Ekow's eldest brother, Fiifi. And then by watching that same brother with the woman he'd lived for and eventually died with.

Fiifi's relationship with Esi had been a melodramatic tragedy to challenge the most epic historical love saga— starting with her being forbidden fruit because their families were sworn enemies, then swerving into the volatile nature of their relationship. He'd never seen two people so right and yet so wrong for each other, their highs and lows a dizzying spectacle he'd watched from a safe and highly sceptical distance.

Of course it had been heartbreaking but almost karmic to witness it end dramatically in a car crash on Fiifi's twenty-fifth birthday, with a lovers' row after a night of ferocious celebration. A shocking tragedy that had rocked both families.

And then there was Ekow's relationship with his father. Or, more accurately, the distinct *lack* of one.

He'd known all that sixteen months ago, during his business trip to South Africa. Yet none of those warnings had made a blind bit of difference while he'd been with her.

Because she left you.

Was he so shallow to let a rejection affect him for this long? Aggravate him this intensely? Or was it something else? Something about *her*?

Evangeline.

Was it because she'd never told him her full name, perhaps? That he wasn't even sure if the first name she had given him was correct? Even while he'd been cynically confident he wouldn't be ensnared by her air of mystique—deliberate, he suspected—he'd ended up yearning to know every single thing about her…

Impatient with his train of thought, he gritted his teeth and surged to his feet. He hadn't thought about her in weeks. And he had more pressing matters to deal with than a woman he was sure would've turned out to be just as ordinary as the rest of them.

'I want a report in the next four hours of who is toying with my security. Fail me and you will be terminated,' he grated into the phone.

Control reinstated, Ekow ended the call and resumed his work day, dismissing the mystery woman from his mind with the same ruthless efficiency with which he ran his family bank.

The report arrived in two hours.

Another hour later and he had the right people in place to track down his hacker.

But some problems required the personal touch, and so Ekow found himself reaching for the phone one final time, and summoning his pilot to ready his jet—destination Cape Town.

He'd deal with this problem once and for all in the

only way he knew how—with Quayson power and might.

And if he was heading to the same city as Evangeline, the woman who'd given herself to him in ways that still stopped his breath and then disappeared without a trace, what did it matter?

CHAPTER ONE

'JONAH, DID YOU hear me? I said dinner is—'

Evangeline Annan froze in the doorway of her brother's room, mild dread seizing her as she watched him scramble around the tiny desk in his room before facing her, his thin-lipped, now-permanent scowl fully in place.

'How many times do I have to tell you to knock before you come in?' he demanded, belligerent even while attempting to wipe the look of guilt from his face.

Evangeline pursed her lips, the worry gnawing at her insides intensifying. 'The door was already open—and, no, that wasn't a suggestion that you lock it from now on. You're fifteen, and the rules—'

'I know what the rules are! "No locking doors in this house,"' he parroted in a voice on the cusp of breaking.

He finally straightened and she felt a pang of mingled pride and sadness. Pride because she'd had a hand in raising this boy who now towered over her, and had succeeded in keeping him alive despite the dire challenges they'd faced. Sadness because her mother hadn't lived to see the man he would eventually become. *If* whatever secrets he was keeping from her didn't land him in worse trouble than the one-week school suspension he'd already incurred in the last academic year.

'What's going on?' she forced out, despite her senses screaming at her to leave it alone.

She'd been a teenager once, and knew that surging hormones, anxiety and finding one's place in the world didn't always make for good bedfellows. Add the death of their mother two years ago, after a long, debilitating and costly illness, and then the very real threat of losing the only home he'd ever known, and it was no wonder her brother had retreated into himself.

Despite all that, though, her baby brother had been extra closed-off in recent months, and while they hadn't been super-close because of their twelve-year age difference, the changes in him felt like night and day, and her sense that there was something wrong wouldn't let up.

On cue, he rolled his eyes. 'There's nothing wrong. Quit the mother hen routine, would you, sis?' he admonished, with a hard bite that hit her in the raw.

He brushed past her on his way to the tiny dining room in the tiny house they shared in Woodstock, on the outskirts of Cape Town city. She knew he'd wolf down his food and dash back into his room within minutes, leaving her torn between giving him his space and attempting further communication.

She followed on slower feet, wondering whether there was another reason for his belligerence.

The thought pulled her focus in a different direction. She bit her lip and glanced towards the closed door of her bedroom. As she'd come to expect, her heart flipped over with awe, love, and the lingering dose of anxiety that constituted being a mother.

Especially a mother to a child whose father had denied every trace of his existence.

Her heart lurched. She breathed through the pang of disquiet and churning emotions dwelling on the man who'd fathered her baby triggered.

This wasn't about her beloved seven-month-old son and the circumstances surrounding his conception and birth.

This was about Jonah.

Entering the dining room, she glanced at her brother. Was he resentful of his new nephew? Resentful that he no longer had Evangeline all to himself?

She shook her head.

No. Jonah adored his nephew.

But it had been just them against the world for so long. They'd been through hell and back, fighting to stay together, fighting to keep the roof over their heads while looking after their sick mother.

That sort of experience should've bonded them, shouldn't it?

'Jonah, whatever is going on, you know you can talk to me, don't you?'

'Sure. Whatever,' he grunted around a mouthful of tuna pasta bake, almost bringing a smile to her face.

But immediately worry wiped it away. 'Are you in trouble?' She mentally crossed her fingers, her breath held, as first outrage and then impatience weaved over his face. 'Because if you're hiding something from me that you shouldn't—'

'You mean like you hid your pregnancy from me for months? Because if anyone knows about keeping secrets it's you, right?' he threw back at her.

They both froze in the ensuing silence, and for a moment remorse flashed in his eyes. Then he brazened it out, shrugging as he went back to eating.

Evangeline swallowed, her fingers curling over the back of the chair across from him. It wasn't the first time her brother had brought this matter up, but it didn't lessen the pain.

'I've told you why I didn't tell you when it happened,' she replied, her lips barely moving.

'Oh, yes—you didn't want to worry me. Because I'm just a useless child, right?'

She sighed. 'Of course not. I mean, okay…yes, you are a child, but that wasn't why.'

'Okay, then, here's your chance. You didn't tell me you were knocked up until you were almost four months pregnant with Leo. Are you going to tell me who the father is or that another secret too?' he asked, one eyebrow raised cockily.

In moments like these, when she got a snapshot of the man he would become even while remnants of his boyishness lingered, she wanted to freeze time, hold the picture in place for ever.

His protectiveness would've been adorable if he hadn't been staring at her with aggrieved hurt.

It was her job to protect him, not the other way around. Which was why she'd used bulky sweaters and loose clothing to keep her pregnancy secret for as long as possible. It had also helped that she hadn't really started to show until well into her second trimester.

'It doesn't matter who he is—'

'Why do you keep saying that? Of course it matters! It'll matter to Leo when he's old enough. Remind me again—which one of us constantly demanded to know who our fathers were before Mum got sick and used that as an excuse not to tell us? You wanted to know, so why is this different?'

'Look, this is nothing to do—' She stopped herself, but knew she'd already said enough when his features tightened.

He scraped back his chair and rose. 'It's nothing to do with me? Well, then, what I do in my spare time is nothing to do with *you* either!'

'Jonah…'

Her conciliatory tone fell on deaf ears as he stalked down the hallway and disappeared into his room.

A quick glance showed he'd eaten every scrap of his meal, and again she would've smiled had the distance between them not seemed so impassable.

Rounding the table, she picked up his empty plate and took it into the kitchen. His accusation stung, but how could she tell him about that weekend?

How could she tell him she'd made a huge error of judgement and landed herself exactly where she'd sworn she'd never be, after witnessing the turmoil and strife her mother had gone through as a single parent? Witnessing the doors closed to her once her family circumstances were discovered…?

According to her mother, she'd been a manager in a small hotel when she'd met and had a brief affair with a businessman, resulting in Evangeline's birth. Then, twelve years later, history had repeated itself and Jonah had been born.

Even on her deathbed her Ghanaian-born mother had refused to tell her and Jonah who their fathers were, citing everything from memory loss to an insistence that Eva and Jonah were better off not knowing.

All Eva had known for certain from her own skin tone and hair was that her father was white. For years she'd been hurt, and then furious with her mother for not divulging her father's identity.

Now, having had her own child, she was still furious, but she had a thin, grudging understanding as to why her mother might have chosen to stay silent. Because if Eva's circumstances were any indication…

With another sigh, she placed her own dinner in the fridge and left the kitchen, her appetite gone.

At the end of the hallway she turned her bedroom door handle slowly and peeked into the room, her heart melting when she saw her son sprawled on his back, his chubby arms and legs spread wide as he slept in his crib.

She'd loved Leo even before she'd seen his tiny feet kick on the ultrasound image at her second prenatal check-up. She had painstakingly taken care of her health in the nine months she'd carried him. And she'd fallen head over heels all over again the moment he'd been placed in her arms.

She'd known then she'd fight to her last breath to protect him from harm or heartache. She didn't care that he was the product of a one-weekend stand. That, like her mother, she'd turned a blind eye to the flashing warning signs telling her she was getting in over her head in waters she'd never swum in. That the kind of overwhelming passion and desire surging through her that weekend was the kind to leave an indelible mark on her.

And, good heavens, had it ever?

Shutting the door, she trudged her way past the

kitchen and into the covered porch overlooking the small garden. She took a deep breath, hoping the slightly humid Cape Town air would disperse the memories.

But, no… They came thick and fast.

Those unnerving few months of uncertainty as to whether Pieter, her boss at the accounting firm where she'd worked, was actually covertly harassing her sexually or—as he'd sardonically stated when she'd mentioned it—it was all in her head.

Then had come his surprise invitation to dinner one Friday after work, to discuss her recent appraisal and a possible promotion. It had followed straight on the heels of her visit to HR, incidentally—which should've cemented her suspicions.

She'd been euphoric that her hard work was being recognised, that she might soon earn enough to afford to pay a few outstanding bills, buy new clothes and educational supplies for Jonah, perhaps eventually move him to a good school, where his computing genius would be better harnessed.

Evangeline had been overwhelmed when Pieter had taken her to the Quayson Cape Town Hotel—*the* most stunningly iconic and luxurious hotel in the city— where A-listers and royalty were rumoured to stay within its sublime spaces.

She hadn't realised just how wrong she'd been until it was too late and all her hopes had crashed and burned at the feet of her lecherous boss and his wandering hands. It had driven her to the bar, straight after she'd thrown her drink in his face and unceremoniously quit on the spot.

Reality had crashed hard on her within minutes.

Even in those incandescent moments after she'd walked away she'd known she'd played right into his hands. That by not staying and fighting she'd done herself and her feminist values a disservice.

Newly jobless, and disappointed in herself for her erratic behaviour, she'd been on the point of angry, frustrated and increasingly anxious tears when she'd hopped onto a bar stool and ordered a stiff rum and Coke. The need to drown her sorrows had made her swallow half the contents at once, grimacing as the bracing liquor seared her throat on its way down.

And then she'd looked up.

Evangeline hated to invoke clichés, but when the most beautiful man you'd ever seen was staring at you when you were feeling at your worst, and his eyes were promising delivery from the depths of the despair you'd blindly tumbled into, you could excuse yourself a cliché or three.

Granted, she'd probably been a touch tipsy, seeing as she wasn't a regular drinker and hadn't eaten all day, naively anticipating the dinner her now *ex*-boss had promised her. The drink had gone straight to her head, doing its job of finding an outlet for said despair.

She'd stared at the drop-dead hot stranger, who'd managed to perch on a stool at the far end of bar as if he owned every man, woman and stick of furniture in sight.

Of course she'd discovered later that his family did indeed own the hotel, along with many more awe-inspiring, successful business ventures.

Unfortunately she hadn't been brazen enough to step down from the stool and sashay her way over to him in that sexy and sultry way she'd seen in the risqué movies she liked to watch. Instead, her fingers had tightened on her glass, the exquisitely carved crystal digging into her flesh, and her every heartbeat had pounded loudly in her ears as he'd returned her brazen stare.

A type of heat she'd never experienced had invaded her system, announcing boldly that she was in the throes of sexual desire. That the stranger at the end of the bar wanted her. And that she wanted him back. *Badly.*

The shocking realisation had shot through her, potent and bewildering enough to whip her focus away from him before he witnessed just how he affected her.

For several seconds she'd stared into her drink, wondering if it was the alcohol having this unusual effect on her. When she'd concluded that the rum definitely didn't help, and that she needed to stop drowning her sorrows and leave, she'd pushed the glass away, her shaky legs thankfully holding her up when she'd slid off the stool.

There had been three exits from the bar—one through the restaurant she'd just come from, another leading to the spectacular atrium and reception area, and a third leading directly onto a quiet side street.

Evangeline had told herself she'd chosen the third door because it was the one nearest to the bus stop for the bus she needed to take her home, not because it would take her past the handsome stranger. Or because it would give her one last glimpse of him before she stepped out into the rainy July evening.

She'd been quietly stunned when her hips had seemed to sway of their own accord, her spine straightening, shoulders squaring and her chin lifting as she made her way down the length of the bar.

She'd been fiercely glad she was wearing her most chic black wraparound dress with its deep V-neck design, its skirt skimming just above her knees, and matching black heels. And that she'd touched up her make-up just before leaving work and her usual fly-away hair was pinned in a neat chignon.

Her professional life might have just been detonated, but at least she could take pride in her appearance. Especially in the presence of the viscerally masculine man who…*dear God*…looked even better up close.

The deep awareness spiralling through her had almost made her stumble. Exhaling in relief when she hadn't, she'd tightened her fingers on her handbag, dragged her gaze from the perfect symmetry of his face, and was forcing herself to take one more step away from him when he spoke.

'Are you really going to let this moment pass?'

Those rumbled words, directed at her but spoken without lifting his gaze from his glass, sounded as if he was mildly offended she hadn't stopped, perhaps come on to him—probably something women had been doing since he hit puberty. They had stopped her dead in her tracks.

'Excuse me?' She hadn't stuttered, for which she'd been immensely grateful, considering the edges of her vision were mildly fuzzy and her heart was beating much too fast.

He'd cracked a ghost of a smile—which, impossibly, had made him even more compelling. 'Is this a run-of-the-mill thing for you, then?' he'd rasped, his eyes scouring her face in a vivid, captivating scrutiny that had made her heart beat even faster, before returning his gaze to his glass.

'Is what?'

The sentence had sounded grammatically off in her brain, but she'd shrugged inwardly. She would toss that into the disastrous dumpster fire this whole evening had turned into—along with her professional life.

His nostrils had flared a little then, as if he wasn't sure whether to be amused or irritated with her. 'Invoking this level of...*stimulation* everywhere you go?'

Evangeline had licked her lips, the stressed word firing up a blaze in her blood and transmitting far too enthusiastically to her groin. It had been as if she was caught in some mysterious sexual vortex, one only he could free her from. And in that moment, when something close to traitorous relief had coursed through her because *he'd* been the one to make her stop, and she was only being well-mannered enough to stop and respond when someone spoke to her, she wasn't entirely sure she wanted to be free.

'I don't... I don't think you can hold me responsible for...for whatever it is you're feeling.'

'Ah, but I do.'

She'd summoned a light laugh—from where, she didn't know. 'Does that pick-up line work with anyone? At all?'

He'd raised his head again then, speared her with a soulful gaze so deep and incisive and all-consuming she'd gasped. If she'd been compelled before, she was completely enthralled in that moment. Looking away had felt like sacrilege—as if she would miss something pure and vital and fundamental, a once-in-a-lifetime phenomenon, if she so much as blinked.

'Forget about anyone else,' he'd rasped, those eyes fixed on her face with such ferocity she'd felt it all the way to her soul. 'Ask yourself why you're still standing there if you're unaffected.'

She'd sucked in an audible breath—because she *had* been affected. Some entity had taken her over, keeping her rooted to the spot, trapped in his electrifying orbit. 'I was just on my way home,' she said. 'And *you* addressed *me*,' she tagged on, proud and grateful to be able to proffer that fact.

He'd scrutinised her face again, as if digging for some truth beneath her skin. 'Yes, I did. And you haven't answered me yet.'

Are you going to let this moment pass?

She should have let it pass. But the lifesaving *yes* had remained locked in her throat. And then he'd risen to his feet, and she'd compounded her circumstances by swallowing the word down.

Well over six feet, with shoulders that blocked out everything else—including her common sense—he had been truly overwhelming. In an almost melodramatic way that made her wonder why he was talking to her, an ordinary girl with an ordinary, if challenging, life.

When he'd wheeled away to address the bartender, Evangeline had reminded herself to breathe.

'Inform the maître d' that I'll take my usual table, and set another place for my guest.' As the bartender had sauntered off to do his bidding he'd turned back to her. 'You *are* staying for dinner, aren't you?'

It had been a sultry invitation and a dare.

A promise of unspeakable pleasure and a warning.

She should've heeded the danger and stepped away from the temptation.

'Only judging by the short and...*interesting* time you spent in the dining room, you've yet to have dinner,' he'd added, one silky eyebrow rising in amused query.

Heat had crept into her face. 'You...you saw me?'

'I think everyone on the ground floor saw you,' he replied. 'It was quite the performance.'

But she didn't care about anyone else. Just *him*. Every racing thought—and there were many in those charged minutes—circled back to him.

While the tipsiness had receded enough for her to make a cogent decision, she'd been getting steadily intoxicated on other things.

His presence. His face. His voice.

The sublime body packed into a bespoke suit.

She'd been about to fall in with his wish, and with whatever else he wanted besides, when a sliver of common sense had arrived, along with a reminder of why she'd been at the bar in the first place. Why she needed to head home to plan for what came next.

He'd followed the glance she'd cast over her shoulder. 'If you're worried about your companion, don't be.'

'He is...*was* my boss. He made a pass at me and I... Well, you saw what I did.'

The glint in his eyes before his jaw clenched tight had been almost...*admiring*. 'Rest assured that I've had him thrown out with a firm recommendation never again to grace this hotel with his dubious presence.'

Evangeline suspected now that *that* was the moment she'd decided to throw caution to the wind. The enigmatic stranger had taken care of one problem without even knowing her name. He'd made her feel better and hadn't mentioned it until she'd needed that tiny little win.

'So what's it going to be?'

The low, unbridled intensity in his voice had sent shivers through her body. And before she could talk herself out of it, she'd responded, 'I'll stay.'

The dark satisfaction gleaming in his eyes should've been further warning that she was playing way out of her league. But, as if he'd known that somewhere inside she was quaking with uncertainty, he'd slowly stepped forward, making her almost swallow her tongue at the sight of his sheer masculinity as he'd held out his arm.

And waited.

Jonah had been away for the weekend at school camp, the only thing awaiting her at home the cold, stark reality of the abrupt ending of a job she'd loved and the shock she was certain she was suffering.

She hadn't been ready to face it. Tomorrow would be soon enough to work out how she'd afford rent and food for her and Jonah once her meagre savings ran out.

So she'd slid her arm into the breathtaking stranger's and let him lead her out of the bar.

They'd been shown into a private dining room— a cosy, stylish space, dripping with the sort of high-quality tasteful decor she only saw on TV shows and in glossy magazines.

But soon enough everything—the superb food, the excellent wine, even the conversation which had contained far too many intoxicating subtexts—had receded from her consciousness.

She'd been wholly and utterly captivated by him.

And it'd seemed like the most profound, transcendent unfolding of a dream when he'd asked her to spend the weekend with him and she'd said...*yes*...

Evangeline squeezed her eyes shut, fighting memories that even now had the power to move a peculiar blend of bewilderment and lust through her body. To turn her nipples diamond-hard and punch heat into her pelvis. To make her clench her fists and drop her head against the windowpane as ravenous need clawed through her. To quietly infuriate her with the knowledge that there'd been no man before or since him. Hell, even the mere thought of dating made distaste sour her mouth.

Because once she'd snapped out of the hypnosis he'd cast upon her a few weeks later, she had been confronted with the harsh reality that he'd left her with an indelible reminder.

Her lips twisted.

And it had just been a small taster of what tangling with Ekow Quayson had in store for her.

Jonah wanted to know who the father of her baby was. But Evangeline knew how headstrong her brother was. Knew he wouldn't rest until he'd forced Ekow to acknowledge Leo the way Jonah's own father hadn't ever acknowledged *his* existence.

She intended to protect Leo from that with every bone in her body.

Because her own attempt to do the same for her son had reaped disastrous results.

Reaffirming to herself that she'd done the right thing by not telling her brother, and that whatever strain there was between them would be overcome in due course, she headed back to the kitchen. She needed to eat, to keep herself healthy. She'd be no use to her family or the treasured clients she'd managed to secure for her small but growing online accounting business if she made herself sick.

She'd just hit the one-minute button on the microwave to warm up her food when she saw the headlights swinging into her small drive.

It wasn't late, but she wasn't expecting anyone. Definitely no one who'd call in after eight p.m.

Evangeline reassured herself that the jump of dread in her stomach didn't mean anything. It was most likely a driver who'd taken a wrong turn.

Still, trepidation wove through her body as she went towards her front door, swallowing as a second, and then a third set of headlights pierced the darkness.

Her neighbourhood was low-income, and most of her neighbours used public transport, just as she did—although her mother's old jalopy functioned from time to time when needed.

The few who owned cars definitely didn't have vehicles gleaming with expensive chrome work, like the ones she spotted when she peeked through the curtains.

She jumped as firm footsteps sounded on the paved path leading to her front door. Her gaze flitted to Jonah's door, and she experienced a peculiar dart of gratitude that he was out of sight.

Taking a deep breath, she pulled open the door before her unwanted visitor could knock and disturb the household.

The breath was snatched clean out of her lungs when

her gaze surged up…and up…and collided with the dark brown, piercingly intense eyes of the very man she'd spent the best part of the last half-hour striving to push out of her mind.

Evangeline was aware her mouth was gaping, her eyes probably wide and horrified as she stared at Ekow Quayson.

'Wh-what are you doing here? And how do you know where I live?' She'd moved since her one and only attempt to reach him fifteen months ago. And she most definitely hadn't been given the chance even to state her full name to him, never mind offer anything close to a phone number or an address for him to reach her.

A scathing dressing down about how 'women like her' were the lowest form of life, followed by a hastily scrawled cheque shoved at her from across a massive teak desk and a stark warning never to set foot in the city of her birth again, were all she'd received from the designated member of his family sent to do his dirty work.

Altogether, her audience with Ekow Quayson's father had taken less than five minutes. But it had left her reeling long afterwards.

And she'd heeded the warning, because in the clear light of day, after that heady weekend, she'd seen who she was dealing with. Known the veritable powerhouse of the family she'd entangled herself with.

'Evangeline.'

The sharp rasp of her name sharpened her focus. Staring at him, she got the feeling he was just as stunned as she was. That whatever he'd expected when he'd marched up to her front door it hadn't been her. But he quickly mastered his expression, leaving her wondering if she'd imagined it.

But if he hadn't then what or who *had* he been expecting?

Her heart leapt into her throat and she quickly glanced over her shoulder, the premonition in her gut expanding. It couldn't be Jonah. *Please, God, no.* 'What do you want, Mr Quayson?' she demanded, far more sharply than she'd intended.

His features clenched with displeasure. 'Hardly the way to greet me after all this time, is it?' he mocked with icy arrogance.

Her own anger trailed through her unease. All this time after the way his father had treated her? After Ekow's own complete silence over his son?

'You think you deserve the red carpet? How very like a rich man to believe the world owes him courtesy simply because of the number of zeros in his bank account.'

One eyebrow slowly rose, his eyes narrowing on her face as he stepped closer. 'I suggest you think twice on the tack you want to take with me. Perhaps you haven't yet seen who else I've brought with me?' he breathed, warning stamped into every syllable.

The fact that it took a monumental effort to drag her far too avid gaze from his face—even more arresting then the last time she'd seen it—past those mile-wide shoulders and the streamlined body draped in a sharp bespoke suit that screamed its birthplace of Milan further irritated her.

But she managed it—only to feel the cold hand of dread tightening its hold on her insides.

'Wh-why have you brought the police with you?'

Unlike the first time they'd met, when her voice had held admirably, her words shook. And she hated every second of that weakness. Hated this man's lasting ability to shake the ground beneath her feet so effortlessly.

First with pleasure, then with debilitating cruelty.

'The chief inspector is a friend. He was kind enough to accompany me here. In case of any…unpleasantness.'

He'd stated the position of authority to further rile her. Evangeline knew that. But despite her best efforts her insides did shake, and she felt her palms growing clammy.

'Do you bring the police to visit all your past acquaintances?' she asked, striving for a tone of casual dismissal which surprisingly held.

The slight flare of his nostrils said she'd hit her mark. But she was too riled to derive any satisfaction from it.

'When they attempt to cause me this level of aggravation, yes,' he returned, in a low, rumbling voice, sending shivers dancing over her skin.

'What are you talking about?'

He didn't answer immediately. He conducted a lazy but thorough scrutiny of her body, reversing her shivers into tiny little sparks of fireworks.

She knew her body hadn't changed that much after childbirth, except maybe in slightly thicker hips and a fuller bust. But she felt as if every inch of her skin had reawakened under his regard.

'Do you live alone?' he continued in his distant thunder voice, and this time there was an edge to his demand that sped up her already racing heart.

'Why?'

His eyes flicked over her shoulder and it was all she

could do not to follow his gaze down the hall. 'Because otherwise it seems I've travelled a few thousand miles to discover that *you* are behind the problems I'm having. For the sake of our past...*connection* I'm willing to hold off the handcuffs and hear you out. So invite me in, Evangeline.'

Memories of pleasurable restraints made of expensive silk ties threatened to crater her thoughts. She furiously shook them away.

'Not until you tell me what you think I've done to lead you to my door. And most definitely not until you send the police away. I'd rather not have a conversation with you while the authorities hang out in my front garden.'

His lips twisted. 'If you're worried about police scrutiny then you shouldn't have hacked into my bank, should you?'

Her shocked gasp dropped into the space between them. 'What? I have no idea what you're—' She snapped her mouth shut far too late.

His sizzling gaze fixed on her face, his eyes slowly narrowing at her unguarded response. 'Then I'll ask you again. Do you live alone, Evangeline?'

She opened her mouth just as the door down the hall opened. And she couldn't quite hide her soft groan of despair as understanding finally dawned.

Before her, Ekow's face turned tight with fury and censure, as if the discovery that she didn't live alone was a black mark against her. He continued to glare at her as footsteps drew closer.

'What's going on?'

Jonah's voice, unmistakably that of a still-growing

boy, drew Ekow's sharp gaze over her shoulder. She saw the wheels turning in his head. Watched his formidable censure begin to recede.

'Eva…?'

The less confident demand from Jonah finally made her turn.

His terrified gaze was fixed on the police cars crouched on their driveway, but it was the guilt on his face when his gaze darted to the police inspector now stepping out of his car which sealed her fears.

'Jonah? What have you done?'

He didn't answer her. She watched him gulp, then gather the jagged edges of his courage before turning his focus on Ekow, animosity brimming in his eyes.

'Jonah!'

She barely registered Ekow turning away from her, taking a few steps to murmur to the police inspector. The older man levelled a reproving gaze on Evangeline for several seconds before, nodding, he returned to his vehicle.

The breath she took didn't quite stem the alarm flaring inside her as Jonah shrugged, shoved his hands deep into his pockets and attempted not to look relieved at the sight of the departing police officers.

'Do not take the absence of the authorities to mean my presence here is benign, Evangeline. One simple phone call can reverse that.'

Evangeline swung back to him. 'No! I… You don't need to do that.'

He nodded, his eyes resting on her face in blatant expectation until she cleared her throat and said, 'Come in.'

The moment Ekow Quayson stepped into her house,

her sanctuary, she regretted inviting him in. Not because she dreaded what was to come—and she did—but because she knew she'd never be able to step into her living room again without recalling his towering presence there. Without seeing him stride past her, his sharp eyes taking in every item of furniture and personal knick-knack before, brimming with disapproval, he turned to her.

'Firstly, you will tell me who this is,' he said, nudging his chin at Jonah. 'And then you'll tell me which one of you is responsible for the breaches in my bank's security. And make no mistake: before I leave here, whoever is responsible will be held accountable.'

CHAPTER TWO

EKOW HADN'T BEEN altogether surprised when the woman who'd taken up far too much space in his brain lately had materialised in front of him.

He'd accepted even before he'd boarded his plane that at some point during his trip to Cape Town he would track her down and pinpoint exactly why she intrigued him so much before walking away.

Of course he hadn't expected to meet her under *these* circumstances. The name his investigation had thrown up was Jonah Annan.

But what really stunned him as he stood in the depressingly tiny living room containing shabby furniture, Evangeline and a glowering teenager, was the rush of hunger, the hard thumping in his chest he realised with alarm was an elevated heartbeat. And the sense of... *anticipation* topping it all off.

The equally unsettling thoughts following fast on the heels of those initial reactions further alarmed him. Sixteen months was a long time between liaisons. The idea that Evangeline, whose surname he now knew was Annan—a Ghanaian name, which absurdly pleased him—could be attached to another man perturbed him.

His gaze darted to her hand, but the punch of relief at seeing her bare fingers was fleeting. The lack of a wedding ring didn't mean much these days. Someone in this house could have a claim on her.

Even confronted with this teenage boy whose features suggested a familial bond, he couldn't quite stem the unnerving sensation. He looked too old to be her son, but that didn't mean she didn't have a significant other on the scene.

'This is Jonah, my younger brother,' she offered eventually.

And just like that Ekow's attention was re-captivated. Just like on the evening in the hotel bar. Just like every second he'd spent with her from then on.

But he couldn't let himself be swayed by the crushed ice and caramel voice that promised sweetness and yet held dangerous edges that could cut a man deep. It was merely one more tool in her alluring arsenal.

He remembered vividly how their weekend had ended.

He turned his attention to the boy. 'Do you know who I am, Jonah?'

The boy shrugged, and a look passed between the siblings. He watched Eva's eyes widen in surprise, while the boy's lips pursed.

'I'll take that as a yes, shall I?' Ekow said, then turned to her. 'Unless you're an accomplished actress, your surprise when I mentioned my bank's security being hacked tells me you know nothing about this?'

A flash of fury was quickly smothered by alarm. 'Of course not. Do you think I'd condone such a thing?'

Ekow's jaw clenched tight before he answered. 'I

have no idea what you'd condone. Our getting to know one another was cut rather short, if I recall accurately,' he stated.

She sucked in a quick breath, sending her brother a fleeting look before glaring at him. When she didn't reply, Ekow let loose a grim smile. 'Or am I not supposed to mention that we know one another?'

Instead of responding, Ekow watched her turn to her brother.

'Is what he's saying true?' she asked. 'Have you been tampering with his bank?'

Jonah snorted. 'I don't *tamper*.' He spat out the word as if it offended him.

'Answer the question, Jonah.' Her gentle tone had attained a ring of steel Ekow would've found impressive had he not still been reeling from seeing this woman in the flesh, sixteen months after she'd left his bed. After he'd been dealt a blow to his ego he wasn't sure he'd quite recovered from.

The young boy shrugged again—a reaction Ekow was recognising was his go-to crutch. 'Answer your sister,' he commanded.

Jonah froze, before his face turned rigid with mutiny. 'So what if I poked around your firewall occasionally? It's not as if I did anything bad. If anything, you should be thanking me for exposing the weaknesses in your system—'

'Jonah!'

'Trust me, you'll be showing me exactly that and more before we're done here,' Ekow announced briskly.

Eva rounded on him, alarm flaring in her eyes. 'What's that supposed to mean?'

'It means now I know I've got the right address and the culprit, you and I are going to talk about reparation. And make no mistake. The penalty will be steep. Your brother is going to walk my team through exactly how he breached my security.'

'Are you saying they don't know? You mean all your billions couldn't buy you adequate protection?' the boy taunted with a smirk, earning himself another fierce glare from his sister.

'That's enough, Jonah,' she said, firmly enough to make him deflate a little.

'Your sister and I need to talk. Excuse us,' Ekow said.

Jonah drew out his obedience for a handful of seconds. Then, with another speaking look at his sister, he started to walk away. Halfway down the hall, he spun around. 'Aren't you even going to ask me why I did it?'

Beside him, Evangeline tensed, then swallowed, as if she was attempting to stem the nerves evidently eating at her. Ekow redirected his gaze to her brother, assessing the teenager's face and his neat but threadbare clothing before he replied, 'You don't look the "hacktivist" type, so I'm going to assume you were just bored.'

The expression that shrouded the boy's face was one decades older than his teenage years. It spoke of a fierce protectiveness buried under all the bravado and acidic fury. And Ekow realised instantly that he was wrong. Whatever had fuelled the young man's desire to toy with his cyber security, it hadn't been done out of boredom but something powerful.

Ekow frowned inwardly. His motive seemed almost...*personal*. Meaning what, exactly?

He focused as Jonah fully faced him, dislike blazing in his eyes. 'Guys like you always assume stuff like that. No, sir, I did it because—'

'It doesn't matter why he did it,' Eva interrupted hurriedly, physically placing herself between them.

Ekow felt a pang of irritation. He was many things, but he wasn't an ogre who went around terrorising women or children. If anything, these two should be begging his forgiveness for their transgressions, not making him feel he was in the wrong for finally tracking down the source of the breaches in his bank.

'I'm sure he's sorry and will work with you on whatever reparations are needed. Won't you, Jonah?' she encouraged pointedly.

Another look passed between them. Ekow swallowed a growl at the increasing certainty that he was missing vital information.

With another careless shrug, the boy sauntered off without answering, walked through a doorway into what Ekow assumed was his bedroom and slammed the door behind him.

Ekow watched Eva stare at the closed door for several seconds, her face a picture of frustration and worry. Her gaze shifted to the second door at the end of the corridor and she swallowed. Then, hastily diverting her gaze, she faced him.

And Ekow felt the punch of lust all over again.

Impossibly, the time between their last meeting and this had added layers of allure to her beauty. Her sultry eyes held mysteries he wanted to uncover. Her unpainted lips seemed even fuller than before, and he was struck with a ravenous hunger to take them, to hear that moan he remembered in his dreams echo in real life.

As for her body…

She might be wearing a pair of worn denim cut-offs and a simple spaghetti-strap top, but the denim clung to her curves, her full hips and rounded buttocks, and her full breasts reminded him of every second he'd spent exploring the silky richness of her skin, discovering which caress made her gasp, which location to linger on with his lips to make her moan.

The high scarlet gloss she'd worn on her fingernails that night might be non-existent now, but he recalled how arousing it had been to feel them digging into his back as he'd taken her again and again. Her scream of pleasure when she'd found her release.

Ekow wasn't aware he was moving towards her until her nostrils quivered and her eyes widened.

'Wh-why are you looking at me like that?' she rasped.

He had pushed his hands into his pockets, much as Jonah had done minutes ago, to stop himself from reaching out to touch her. Reacquainting himself with the cushiony softness of her plump lips.

'Why did you sneak out of my bed before I got the chance to learn your full name?' he grated, and then froze.

The words had surprised him almost as much as they evidently did her, but once the question was spoken he knew the answer was one he'd been seeking for sixteen months.

Her beautiful eyes widened even further. '*That's* what you want to talk about? I thought you were here because—'

'We'll get to your brother's transgressions and your role in them in due course. Tell me why.'

'I don't owe you an explanation—and what do you mean by my role in them? I had no idea he was doing… whatever it is you think he's done.'

'Which either means you're shockingly inattentive or you just wilfully turned a blind eye to what was happening under your own roof.'

'How dare you!'

Just as he remembered from the incident in his restaurant at their first meeting, her fiery animation drew him like a vivid beacon. Her spark made him want to step closer, experience her heat. Singe himself raw with it.

Ekow accepted then that whatever else had brought him to Cape Town, the allure and mystery of Evangeline Annan would be an added bonus he would unravel before he returned to Accra.

But first things first… 'I dare because his actions have cost me a couple of million dollars in security investigation fees.'

She gasped. 'I…that's not possible.'

'Are you calling me a liar, Eva?'

Her lips pursed. 'If you think I'm just going to take your word for it, then, no, I'm not going to. I'll need proof of what you're accusing Jonah of.'

'Even though he just as good as admitted it?'

She sent a fleeting glance over her shoulder, then squared both those gorgeous shoulders. 'Like you said, he's a teenager. Maybe he tinkered around a time or two on your bank's website, but that doesn't—'

'He's been doing it for eight months, Evangeline,' he corrected, fresh irritation storming through him.

She gasped. 'No…'

'Yes. And he did much more than tinker. Shutting down my systems for a few hours and sending pictures of picnicking cats to all my board members isn't a laughing matter.'

A look of deeper trepidation settled on her face. 'He didn't do anything more…banking specific, did he?'

'Are you asking me whether he stole money from my bank?'

She froze for several seconds, then exhaled shakily. 'Did he?'

'Fortunately for him, no, he didn't.'

Her shoulders sagged in relief.

Ekow's lips thinned. 'Don't break out in thankful song yet, sweetheart. He's still committed multiple cybercrimes—both here in South Africa and in Ghana.'

'Is that why you've come here? To cart my fifteen-year-old brother off to jail?'

He'd most definitely come because he wanted to get to the root of a problem which should've been dealt with months ago if the cyber thief hadn't been so slippery. But discovering Eva's connection to the boy threw a different light on things. The sense that something else was going on with Jonah, at least. Perhaps with them both.

'I haven't made up my mind yet.'

'I won't have you toying with him. Or me,' she warned, her beautiful chin tilted up in fierce defiance.

'Not even if accommodating me might earn you a path to my better, more lenient nature?'

Suspicion filled her eyes. 'Accommodating you in what way?' she demanded.

He delivered a mirthless smile. 'Not in the way you think. I've never needed to seek sexual favours in return for co-operation or anything else. I believe that was your ex-boss's remit?'

The suspicion drained from her eyes but there remained a fire deep within the dark hazel depths that echoed the one burning low but insistent inside him, triggering a pulse of satisfaction.

'Then what *do* you mean?'

'You can start by telling me why your brother would target me and my bank in this way. Because, whether you want to admit it or not, this feels personal. What are you two hiding from me?'

In the time between Ekow's unwanted arrival on her doorstep and learning of Jonah's online activities Eva had asked herself the same question.

Unfortunately, and alarmingly, everything pointed to her brother having taken it upon himself to punish Ekow Quayson. His comments at the dinner table finally made sense.

While she'd been thinking she was protecting him by not enlightening him about the inauspicious period surrounding Leo's conception, birth and what had happened during her visit to Ghana afterwards, Jonah had been smarting at being kept in the dark. And he'd taken matters into his own hands.

Her brother had always been a whizz kid with computers. She knew in her bones that he'd gone snooping and discovered the truth—or at least enough of it—and attempted to dish out his own retribution.

A small part of her was fiercely proud of his protectiveness. But the major part knew this was a big problem.

Eight months...

She barely stopped herself from shutting her eyes in despair. The formidable man in front of her would still be there when she opened them. His scent would still fill her nostrils, his intoxicating good looks would threaten to blind her despite the fact that with every second that passed without him even asking about his son pain was biting into her chest like steel barbs.

How could she stand there cataloguing his every breathtaking feature when he was the epitome of everything she despised in men? In her book, there was nothing worse than a man who didn't own up to his responsibilities.

Over the years, even though her mother had never admitted it, Eva knew she'd attempted to reach Jonah's father. She'd seen the returned letters and overheard phone calls which had driven her mother to heartbreaking tears in the middle of the night when she'd thought her children were asleep.

Jonah had always been sensitive, and Eva suspected her brother had discovered his own father had rejected the chance to know him. The same course Ekow Quayson had instructed his father to take on his behalf over their son.

Hell, he hadn't even been man enough to tell her to her face that he was rejecting her offer for him to know and love his own flesh and blood. No. He'd left the task to his brutally unforgiving father.

She shivered at the recollection, then welcomed the burn of anger the memory stirred inside her.

'Is that distaste filling your face supposed to mean something to me?' Ekow demanded in a low, deep faintly mocking tone.

Her mouth twisted. Of course her reaction would bounce like water off his formidable shoulders. He was well-insulated by his wealth, power and effortlessly perfect good looks. Men like him felt they only needed to lift a finger to have their problems disposed of. No doubt he'd inherited that trait from his father.

'I'm surprised you chose to come here yourself. Don't men like you have endless minions to solve problems like this for them?'

'You're changing the subject. And you know that will only raise my suspicions, don't you? As for attending to this myself—you should be thankful I did. A subordinate would've been instructed to let the authorities handle this matter and your brother would be in handcuffs by now.'

Something vital quaked inside her but she refused to back down. 'Are you…will you give me your word that you won't involve them?'

He tilted his head to one side, a sardonic look shrouding his face. 'You've been in equal measures belligerent, defiant and downright hostile. Why should I do you any favours, Evangeline?'

Dear God, but the way he said her name made treacherously sinful thoughts invade what should be a clearcut discussion.

Eva admonished herself for that unfortunate reaction and cleared her throat. 'You want to know why Jonah is interested in you? The weekend you and I were… together…he was supposed to be at school camp. But he didn't like it there and he'd been trying to reach me—to ask me to come and get him. When I didn't answer my phone he decided to take matters into his own hands. He ran away and came home early. But I wasn't at home.'

He frowned. 'That was why you left without waking me?'

It wasn't entirely why. She'd already been halfway out the door when she'd received the call from a worried camp supervisor. 'Partly.'

His eyes narrowed. 'We're going to be better acquainted before this issue between us is resolved, so I should mention that I don't like half-answers. What's the other reason that had you leaving my bed at the crack of dawn?'

'Why don't you come out and state what's really bothering you?' she asked him.

He half smiled. 'What makes you think I'm bothered?'

'The way I left you? Isn't that why you're questioning me like this? Because I took away your power over the situation by not staying until you'd formally dismissed me after the weekend was over? I imagine not many women leave without fawning endlessly over you.'

'You imagine correctly,' he replied, without an ounce of self-doubt. 'So why *did* you leave?'

His persistent questioning was the last thing she'd expected. After all, he wasn't a man who needed to preen to get attention. He wasn't a man who had to boast about his masculine beauty and his raw physical prowess.

Every square inch of Ekow Quayson screamed power and authority. Every streamlined muscle had been designed to command the female gaze, so he could glory in having won the genetic lottery that had sculpted a perfect man, who only needed to enter a room to control it. Only to look at a woman to have her in the palm of his hand.

That first night she'd resisted in the final moments between leaving the dining room and going upstairs with him. Lord, had she resisted.

Granted, the event with her boss which had immediately preceded their meeting had inured her somewhat to the raw potency that had hit her the moment she'd laid eyes on Ekow Quayson at the bar of Quayson Cape Town—the sublimely luxurious, six-star hotel she'd discovered, somewhere between her second and third drink, was part of the worldwide hotel conglomerate operated by his family. But still it had only been a matter of time before her resistance had crumbled to nothing.

Before she'd convinced herself that not all men were like her disgusting newly ex-boss. Or the two men who'd sired her and her brother, then left her mother to face the hardships of being a single parent on her own.

Before she'd acted so completely out of character that she still reeled in recollection nearly a year and a half later.

Now she forced an unruffled shrug, despite her stomach churning with fresh warning that things weren't what they seemed. 'I thought I'd spare us both the unnecessary morning-after awkwardness,' she said lightly.

Only to feel her heart flip over in alarm when his jaw tightened and something resembling displeasure shimmered in his eyes before he grappled it down.

Was she mistaken?

Had he, contrary to his very thinly veiled warning for her not to take their weekend as anything above face value, not been thrilled that she'd left his penthouse suite in the early hours of Monday morning while he'd been fast asleep, their sexual antics having worn them both out so completely it had taken huge willpower to force herself to leave?

'Impatient to get on with the rest of your life, were you? I find that hard to believe. Our time together wasn't as forgettable as you pretend—was it, Eva?'

The question held traces of conceit—as if, no matter her response, he'd already made up his mind about their time together and his belief cemented his place as an unforgettable entity in her past…one she'd never be free of.

She pursed her lips, determined not to give him the satisfaction he craved. Because, even without the living, breathing reminder of their encounter currently fast asleep down the hall, Eva knew she would never have forgotten him. Their coming together had been a visceral, earth-shattering event. At least for her.

As for Ekow… He hadn't seemed to dislike it either. Not that she was about to claim any sexual expertise. After all, she'd been a virgin before she'd taken his hand and boarded the lift up to his penthouse that Friday night.

She'd come down to earth a far too enlightened woman. A woman who knew the true depths of physical intimacy… Who knew the touch of a sublime, masterful lover… Who knew she would never be the same… A woman who hadn't been able to bring herself to seek that kind of intimacy elsewhere since.

Perhaps if she hadn't discovered weeks later that she was carrying Leo she would've resented Ekow for ruining all other relationships for her. But her life had taken a drastic turn, leaving her with no option but to focus on the one treasure that mattered.

Her child.

The child she needed to put above all this pointless reminiscing…

'Whether it was forgettable or not, I left on my own terms. That's all the answer you need, isn't it?'

A grim smile cracked across his face. 'No. I never take things at face value or I wouldn't even be here in the first place.'

Another layer of unwanted panic slid into place inside her. 'What's that supposed to mean?'

'It means someone wanted my attention and they made their presence known by interfering with the smooth running of my bank. Tell me the truth. Did your brother act under your instruction?'

She frowned. 'Why would I do something like that?'

He shrugged. 'Perhaps it was your brother acting on his own. The question is why? I don't believe it's his idle curiosity about who you were with that weekend.'

She waved a hand, attempting to render the whole argument inconsequential. 'He's a teenager. They all want attention in some form or another, even though it's the absolute last thing they'll admit to wanting. You're a young, successful billionaire—he's probably convinced he can emulate you in some way. I don't think you should take it too seriously.'

For some reason her response sent another of those mysterious shadows across his face. And, just as before, it was gone almost as soon as it arrived. 'His supposed hero-worship has cost my bank a lot of time and resources—so, no, I'm not simply going to overlook it and walk away.'

'He's a fifteen-year-old boy. What exactly do you hope you'll achieve?'

'At the very least I will impress on him that this kind of course of action might land him in jail, or worse.'

For a fleeting second Eva wanted to confess she wanted to do that too. She hadn't exactly mastered the art of tough love—not when it came to her beloved sibling—and look where it had got them. But then she reminded herself of the ruthless power of the Quaysons. Of what their patriarch had threatened her with when she'd dared to do the right thing. She couldn't expose Jonah to that sort of treatment.

'My investigation has revealed that you operate an online accountancy business from your home,' he said, changing tack.

'Yes, what of it?' she answered briskly, determined not to show how nervous his questions made her.

'You deal with people's private finances while your brother is a prolific hacker?'

His words were so dry Eva imagined the smallest spark would start a blaze.

'I'm sure I don't need to draw you a picture.'

He didn't, and that fact had crossed her mind more than once since he'd turned up. Her freelance business

was still fledgling. She treasured the flexibility it gave
her to raise Leo while earning an income to keep the
roof over her family's head. All it would take was for
word to get out about Jonah's activities and everything
she'd worked so hard for would be jeopardised.

But she was damned if she'd give Ekow the satisfaction of admitting her alarm. 'Are you remotely near
making a point?' she asked. 'Or should I take what you
say as the threat it clearly is?'

Those far too sumptuous lips twisted, as if she
amused him. As if all this turmoil he was causing was
a trifling inconvenience and he was simply taking time
out of his busy day to deal with it.

But it wasn't, though, was it?

He'd boarded his private jet and flown all the way
here to deal with this matter. And there was a watchful
tension about him, a careful examination of each word
she spoke, each look, each tiny movement of her body.

She already knew how powerful he and his family
were. Unless she took control of this she'd find herself
back in the same place she'd been fifteen months ago,
when she'd faced down another Quayson and been un-
equivocally vanquished.

Looking at Ekow now, she saw the visceral resemblance to the older Quayson, and the alarm snaking
through her grew more potent. More vicious.

Surprise flashed through his eyes, and she might've
thought it genuine if she hadn't had an unforgettable
play-by-play of his rejection of their son in her mind.

'Threaten *you*? So far my issue is with your brother.
Why should you and I be enemies?'

She shook her head to dispel its spinning. 'You're joking, right?'

His eyes narrowed. 'Why would I be?'

A waterfall of ice doused her anger, replacing it with deep, deep dread. All along she'd thought his absence from Leo's life was deliberate. That her news had been received with the heavy scepticism and rejection she'd feared, and received confirmation of when she'd made the trip to Accra. But what if—?

'Eva?'

She forced herself to focus on the present. She knew the truth about him, whatever reason he had for wanting to play dumb right now. The son he'd rejected was truly better off without him if he couldn't even be bothered to enquire after him.

Was this how her mother had felt? Why she'd been so bitter and disillusioned for most of Eva's life?

She pushed the thought away.

She needed to handle the matter in front of her and be done with him—hopefully once and for all. 'I'm not sure how your family operates, but to me if you have an issue with my brother, then you have an issue with me.'

That infernal smile made an appearance, although this time it didn't quite reach his eyes. 'My family isn't without its challenges, but I can't say we've ever resorted to trespassing where we're not wanted or dabbled in cybercrime.'

Her shivering intensified. She truly wanted to believe this was all some giant misunderstanding. But the very real presence of the authorities he'd brought to her front door told her she couldn't wish reality away.

Thank God she lived on a quiet street. It was dark

enough for most of her nosy neighbours to have missed this event. If she was lucky.

'It sounds like your brother is more than a handful,' he said into the tense silence.

'I'd thank you not to disparage—'

'It's a frank observation. Take offence if you like, but it won't diminish the truth.'

His words seared her with their honesty. She'd known for a while that she was burying her head in the sand where Jonah was concerned. Nevertheless, hearing it from this man, who'd shirked his chance at fatherhood, struck her as a little too raw, rousing her anger to fiery proportions.

'With respect, your observations mean less than nothing to me. Jonah is my problem, not yours.'

His face hardened, a granite ruthlessness settling over his features. 'That's where you're wrong. He put himself in my crosshairs by messing with my bank. He's now *my* problem.'

'Fine. Go on, then. What hoops do we have to jump through so you can be satisfied?'

For an age, he just stared at her.

Eva felt her skin tightening as apprehension and some emotion she didn't want to entertain slithered through her. It was far too reminiscent of that first time, when he'd stared back at her from across the bar as if he already knew all her secrets. As if her every desire was his to command and satisfy at his leisure.

'Have dinner with me,' he said abruptly.

Her shocked exhalation was the only sound in the room following his demand. Then, 'What?'

He cast a fleeting glance around the room, his eyes

lingering on the dining table she hadn't quite finished clearing. 'It's late tonight. It looks like you've already eaten. I have meetings all day, but I'm free to discuss this tomorrow night. We can have dinner while we do.'

He expected her to sit down and break bread with him after what he'd done to her? Evangeline would've laughed hysterically at his sheer gall had his utterly despicable behaviour not felt so searingly personal. So reminiscent of her mother's heartbreak. Of the fear and uncertainty Eva herself had felt after returning from Accra with his father's threats ringing in her ears and her tail between her legs.

'No, Mr Quayson. My answer is, *hell*, no.'

CHAPTER THREE

SHE WAS DOING it again. Openly displaying the dismissiveness that said she didn't care whether they remained talking or he disappeared in a puff of smoke.

In truth, it was what had intrigued Ekow at their first meeting, when she'd stood up from the bar and walked past him with every intention of leaving.

Sure, she'd had many highly admirable physical attributes which had also caught his attention. But her mild disdain—when everyone else he met went out of their way to ingratiate themselves with him—while she'd been in the process of walking out after that singularly electric connection between them... Yes, it had left him flummoxed.

For the first time he'd *enjoyed* a woman playing hard to get, relished being a true hunter instead of a man whose prey fell willingly into his clutches.

And, yes, it had also produced in him a welcome edge which had cut through his jaded senses, triggered a sharp hunger in him, a man used to feasting whenever he desired.

Put simply, Evangeline's unique blend of innocence and passion had been a refreshing, addictive novelty.

And then, just as quickly as he'd tasted her desire, he'd known one night wouldn't be enough. And had been surprisingly thrilled when she'd agreed to spend the weekend with him.

Had it all been a carefully orchestrated set of events to bring him here, to this moment? In his experience, women who gravitated towards men with billionaire status were willing to go above and beyond to achieve their goals.

But if she wasn't playing a part, he could—

What? Talk her into picking up where they'd left off? Or, more accurately, where she'd left *him*? Stunned, surprisingly dejected, and a little irritated at both feelings. Or was it because he'd woken up craving more of her and having to let that hunger go unsatisfied wasn't an occurrence he'd appreciated?

The sting to his pride had cut deeper than he wanted to admit. And hurt it still did. He was damned if he would grant her the chance to stage a repeat act.

Wouldn't payback be sweet if *he* did the leaving this time? Left her wanting more? It wasn't as if the hunger was one-sided. He'd seen the same flare of awareness in her eyes when she'd opened her front door.

Contrary to Eva's words, she wasn't quite over their torrid weekend together. They had unfinished business. She'd robbed him of something by stealing out of his bed before he'd finished things on his terms.

The more the idea settled in his brain, the more palatable it grew.

It was better than living in limbo.

Limbo was where his father had left him for most of his life. And even in death his old man had ensured his youngest son was left with questions which would haunt him for the rest of his life.

Had he ever done anything to make his father proud, or was he truly the inconsequential 'spare', only useful for the duties no one else in the family had wanted to take on? Even after he'd clawed his way up from lowly intern to managing Africa's largest private bank after his father had stepped down it had only been because the old man was being forced to relinquish control after suffering a series of grave health issues, not because he'd deemed Ekow worthy of the position.

And on his last day on earth he'd asked not for Ekow but for his second son, Atu. His father had hung on until his brother's plane had landed from Malta, then sent Ekow to fetch the heir apparent. It was Atu and his mother who'd been by their father's side when he passed away. Joseph Quayson hadn't even bothered to hang around to bid his youngest son farewell.

A week later he'd discovered he hadn't been worthy of a mention in his father's will either. All his assets had been left to his wife and his second son.

Ekow had been ready to fight to retain control of the bank he'd given his life to, but luckily neither Atu nor his mother had dared to stand in his way.

Some days, though, victory felt hollow, and he despised himself for *still* needing his dead father's endorsement…

He gritted his teeth against the surge of dark, tormenting memories. These days he fought not to dwell on his father unless it was absolutely necessary.

'Hell, no?'

He echoed her answer, steeping himself in the present. Regardless of the ideas he was tossing around in his head about Eva, Jonah had effortlessly breached his bank's firewalls—the last skirmish as recently as last night. *That* was as unacceptable as her answer.

'By all means we can have a discussion about Jonah and what he can do to make things right. But I won't be having it over a cosy dinner, as if we're friends.'

He frowned inwardly at her acerbic tone, then shrugged it off. She could protest all she wanted, but *he* was the wronged party.

'You misunderstand. This isn't a social engagement. We'll be sitting down to discuss the best way forward. I'm a busy man. Come Monday, I'll be flying back to Accra. By then, one of two things will have happened. I will have handed this matter over to the authorities—an outcome I suspect you don't want—or we will have reached an agreement on how to handle this issue privately, between us. Which option would you prefer?'

Her expression indicated she preferred neither. That she wished him as far away from here as was humanly possible. Which also grated. No woman had ever been this conclusively dismissive of him. Usually they fell over themselves for a second date with him.

But not Evangeline.

She'd folded her arms, and her stunning face was set in mutinous lines resembling the expression her brother had flaunted a short while ago. 'Very well. But if I decide to eat with you dinner will be at a place of my choosing,' she stated eventually, her snappish tone disencouraging further disagreement.

'Because…?' he asked anyway, intrigued despite himself at her sheer temerity.

'Because you're about to suggest we dine at your hotel—am I right?'

Since it was the truth, he didn't deny it. 'The Quayson Hotel boasts the best restaurants and chefs in the city. I fail to see what you have against it.'

Her lashes swept down and he felt a moment's satisfaction in a sea of disgruntlement. She wasn't making the demand because she hated the idea of dining with him at the Quayson Hotel. She was doing so because she wasn't quite as indifferent to the memories plaguing him as she wanted him to think.

'Ah…you don't want to be reminded of how uninhibitedly passionate you were with me there that night? Is that it?'

He'd expected her to deny it, coyly or otherwise, like most women who attempted to project one emotion when they felt another. To his surprise, she lifted her stubborn, beautiful chin.

'No, I don't. It was a night I prefer not to remember at all.'

Anger now played second fiddle to another, far superior emotion—the unnerving punch of rejection, chilling and achingly familiar. He told himself it didn't compare to the sensation he'd had to live with growing up, to the endless times his needs had been batted aside by his father. But, alas, there it was, eating its insidious way inside him, reminding him far too efficiently that he'd never been good enough. Never worthy of the care and attention his eldest brother had enjoyed, and even his second brother Atu to some extent. Because, despite their head-butting, hadn't his father been desolate in the weeks after Atu had upped sticks and relocated to the other side of the world, citing his inability to live with their merciless father?

And hadn't he, Ekow, the one left behind, been to all intents and purposes invisible to his father?

Perhaps under different circumstances he would've granted Eva's wish. But a cloying need not to be dragged back into that desolate swamp of indifferent dismissal he'd been subjected to far too often in his life hardened his decision.

'Unfortunately for you, I hold all the cards here, Miss Annan. You will come where I wish and stay for as long I wish. And my wish is that you join me for dinner at the Quayson Hotel.'

Her eyes flared with alarm, sparking the merest twinge of guilt. But it was gone the next instant, and stony defiance was etched into her expression as she returned his stare.

'If throwing your weight about is what strokes your ego enough to get this situation resolved, then so be it.'

He welcomed the spark of triumph that washed away the stench of dejection and allowed himself a smile. 'My ego is perfectly robust and healthy. I'll inform you if it needs tending. I'll pick you up at seven p.m.'

Something resembling angry relief crossed her face. It was peculiar enough to slow his steps to the door. 'And just in case you're thinking of making a run for it, don't bother. I have people watching this house.'

Her head whipped towards the window, then returned to him, her face flushed with her wrath. 'You're not serious!'

Ekow crossed his arms. 'Try spending months wondering who's toying with your bank's security systems and making a fool out of you, and you'll know just how serious I am.'

She batted his words away with an elegant hand. 'I'll be here. I'm not afraid of you, Mr Quayson. Definitely not enough to uproot my life just to hide from you. I didn't do it sixteen months ago and I won't do it now.'

He opened his mouth to demand to know what she was talking about, but she strode past him—and, damn it, he was too distracted by the sway of her hips and the delicious bounce of her rounded buttocks to form the words before she opened her front door.

Hand on the doorframe, she glared at him. 'As for having someone toy with your life—believe me, I know what that feels like. Goodbye, Mr Quayson.'

'Not goodbye, sweet Eva. It's good*night*.'

Her luscious lips firmed and that hard punch of temptation returned, rushing lustful heat through his system. His tongue thickened with the need to taste her. It was all he could do to stride forward, walk out into the sultry Cape Town heat to his town car. And he barely registered the journey, his thoughts playing back over his encounter with Eva.

Sixteen months ago he'd needed a release valve for the thick layer of discontentment cloaking his every interaction. Eva had been it for him. Her sinful curves had literally stopped his breath when he'd seen her stalking out of the restaurant, fury enlivening her magnificent, expressive face.

The evening had unfolded in a way far beyond his expectations. Discontentment had been washed away by raw, mindless sex with a woman whose occasional displays of innocence had perfectly blended with her unbridled passion.

So much so, he'd even contemplated extending what he'd intended to be a two-day affair. He'd planned to ply her with a lavish breakfast on Monday…give her a few more pertinent details beyond his name and his connection to the Quayson Hotel Group and the Quayson conglomerate at large.

He'd decided right before he'd succumbed to sleep that he did, in fact, deserve a vacation.

In the wider professional arena he'd earned accolades, respect, and a bank balance he couldn't spend in several lifetimes. All while dealing with an increasingly ungrateful and ever more indifferent father.

Taking a week, maybe two, out of his busy schedule to unwind in South Africa hadn't sounded like the worst idea in the world. Especially when the woman he intended to spend that time with had dramatically quit her job and sent her wholly undeserving boss packing. Making her a free agent.

The last thing he'd expected was to wake up alone, with no sign of the woman who'd electrified his world.

Ekow slid a contemplative finger over his bottom lip as he eased back in his seat. He hadn't been able to banish her from his mind as he'd wished, but no matter… He'd risen to his enviable position in life because he knew when to grasp opportunities when the timing was right.

And he couldn't help but welcome the one just presented to him.

'You're going out? Let me guess… With *him*?'

Eva flinched at her brother's acerbic tone. She didn't

need to look up from changing Leo's nappy to know he was seriously ticked off.

She exhaled before she answered. 'Yes, I'm going out. Yolanda will be here in half an hour,' she said. 'I'll try not to be late.'

'I don't need a babysitter,' he grumbled, sauntering into the room as she tickled her son's rounded stomach and revelled in his unfettered laughter. 'Why are you going out with him?'

She glanced at him, fighting her irritation. All day she'd tried to get him to discuss why he'd targeted Quayson Bank's security systems. All she'd received were grunts and sullen silences. 'Why do you think? This problem isn't going to go away just because you refuse to talk about it, Jonah.'

He stiffened, then shrugged. 'What's there to say? I messed about with his bank's firewall.'

'You could start by telling me why you did it!'

'You know why,' he tossed back, his face darkening with anger. 'He knocked you up and left you to fend for yourself, just like Mom had to! Someone needed to teach him a lesson. Someone needs to teach them *all* a lesson.'

Her heart dropped. Having her suspicions confirmed chilled her to the bone. 'Jonah, it's not up to you to take matters into your own hands like that.'

'Yeah? Why not? You weren't going to do anything. You were just going to let him get away with it. Let him live his life and do it all over again to some other woman like your father and mine did!'

Leo whimpered, his beautiful hazel eyes growing wider as he picked up on the tension in the air.

She picked him up, brushed a kiss on his cheek as she bounced him in her arms.

'That's enough,' she directed at Jonah, keeping her voice even so her son didn't get even more distressed. 'First of all, my battles are mine to fight—not yours. You don't know the whole story—and, no, I'm not going to tell you, so don't even ask. All I'm concerned about is you and Leo. That you're both healthy and happy and safe. You bringing the authorities to our door risked that, and I wish you hadn't done it.'

His lips twisted but he kept silent.

'Promise me you won't do anything like that ever again,' she pressed.

For an age, he remained mutinously silent. Then he met her gaze. 'I won't mess with his bank if he does the right thing by you.'

She buried her face in her son's curly hair and squeezed her eyes shut, her heart fracturing a little bit more. She knew if she told Jonah the full story he'd be even more livid.

Somewhere along the line, he'd developed a rigid sense of right and wrong. To him there were no grey areas. She loved him for that, but also despaired a little at his complete intransigence.

'I don't need anything from him,' she said eventually. He frowned and opened his mouth, but she beat him to it, holding a babbling Leo out to him. 'Here, look after your nephew. I need to get dressed.'

He eyed the dress on the bed as he took Leo from her. With money being tight, and Eva not needing to dress every day for the office anymore, her work wardrobe had essentially stayed the same in the last few years.

But, as much as she wanted to, she didn't think she'd make the right impression by turning up at the Quayson Hotel in cut-off jeans, a boat-necked sweater and ballet flats.

The black dress she'd worn the night she'd met Ekow remained her most stylish and timeless dress and, while it evoked memories she'd rather not dwell on, it fitted the bill for tonight.

'You're going to dinner with him to discuss me. Shouldn't I be there? To…you know…defend myself?' Despite his belligerence, Jonah cracked a smile when Leo grabbed his cheek.

'I think you've done quite enough, don't you?' Her tone was a little sharp, but she didn't regret it. She'd been far too soft with him. She hardened her heart against the hurt look he cast her.

His lips pursed. 'If he hurts you again…'

Her anger melted away. Going to him, she engulfed both her adored boys in a bear hug, kissing one chubby cheek, then a leaner one. 'He won't. I won't let him. I promise.'

Jonah regarded her for several seconds and then, nodding, he left the room with Leo.

Forty minutes later she was reciting those words to herself as she kissed her baby, said goodbye to her friend and neighbour Yolanda, and shut her front door behind her.

Earlier this afternoon she'd left a message at the hotel to say she would meet Ekow at the restaurant. She'd deliberately not spoken to him directly because she'd feared he would object and turn up at her house anyway. She didn't think she could abide another evening of him invading her space while actively ignoring the son he'd never once acknowledged.

Besides, making her own way there would ensure she approached this evening on her own terms.

The small car she'd inherited from her mother was old, but it still ran well—thanks to Yolanda's husband's mechanical skills and insistence on a free yearly service. About to unlock it, she paused when powerful headlights cut across her front lawn.

Frozen, Eva stared at the luxury town car idling several feet away. Her heart leapt into her throat when the back door opened and Ekow alighted with a suave grace that screamed his class and pedigree. Straightening to his full, towering length, he let his gaze rake leisurely over her.

'What are you doing here?' She ignored the breathlessness in her voice and attempted her fiercest glare.

He looked from her to her car, dismissing it with faint distaste. 'I said I would pick you up.'

'And I left a message saying I would meet you there. I'm sure your staff are competent enough to have delivered it.'

His lips thinned. 'They did. I ignored it. Because you're not going on your own. Especially not in a death trap. Is that rust-bucket even roadworthy?' he sneered.

'There's nothing wrong with my car. It runs perfectly fine.'

'But you won't be using it tonight.'

He waved a hand her towards the sleek town car. She remained where she was, and slowly his face hardened.

'I insist.'

Only the reminder that she needed to keep him on-side if she hoped to gain leniency for Jonah kept her from shoving his insistence in his face. As he'd stated last night, he held the cards. For now.

Dropping her keys back into her clutch, she strutted to the car on heels that felt a little alien since she hadn't worn them in months, and she was entirely too conscious of how much her hips swayed, how her hem brushed her thighs. How she couldn't catch a full breath because of the traitorous awakening occurring inside her at the first whiff of his masculine scent.

What the hell was wrong with her?

She watched him wave away the driver and reach forward to open the door himself. As he straightened he turned his head and their gazes collided.

Evangeline gave a soft gasp at the fire blazing in his eyes. Whatever else was going on, Ekow remained an intensely passionate man, unafraid to show when he found a woman attractive.

And he found her attractive.

No. She was just the tool he'd used to scratch an itch sixteen months ago. One he'd been content to forget despite the life they'd created between them.

She would walk through the flames of hell before she succumbed to even a fraction of what had happened in those forty-eight hours of madness.

If not for her own sake, for the sake of her precious son. For her brother.

She willed rejection into her body, forcing icy coldness into her eyes as she returned his stare.

Slowly, the fire died in his eyes, and the sensual lips she recalled devouring far too vividly thinned into a flat line.

'Get in the car, Eva,' he grated, pulling the door wide open. 'I'm quite eager to understand why you keep directing such hostility at me with those beautiful eyes.'

Her fingers tightened around her clutch as bewildered anger washed away the icy chill. 'I don't understand *you*. In what world do you think it's acceptable to expect me to be civil towards you when you've rejected your own—?'

A child's distressed cry ripped through the evening air, making them both turn around.

Her heart leapt, then dropped sharply, leaving her choking back her own distress. Leo was at that frustratingly adorable age when he rejected everyone and actively threw himself into his mother's arms whenever she was within eyesight.

And her son, having caught sight of her from the front door, was now straining towards her, his plump arms insistently outstretched.

Her gaze shifted to her brother, who stood defiantly on the front porch, his angry gaze fixed on Ekow while he held his nephew.

She squeezed her eyes shut for a calming second.

Jonah knew exactly what he was doing. He might have half-heartedly given his word that he wouldn't meddle any more in Ekow's professional business, but he'd still found a way to force him to acknowledge his son.

Beside her, Ekow froze, his eyes widening as he took in the scene.

Eva's heart leapt into her throat as she watched him set eyes on his son for the first time. Watched him stare. And stare. *And stare.*

His head whipped towards her, and there was shock she didn't believe for one second flashing in his eyes. 'Is there something you want to tell me, Eva?'

Her insides quivered at the granite-hard demand.

'No,' she said, through lips numb with the pain she'd hoped would've healed by now but apparently lay just beneath the surface, waiting to surge up, to remind her not only of the rejection Leo has suffered but her own rejection by the father she'd never met. 'I've wasted enough time trying to do that.'

His eyes narrowed. 'What the hell is that supposed to mean?' he breathed.

Leo cried out again.

Jonah stepped off the porch, his slow strides bringing him closer. She wanted to scream at him to take her baby boy back inside. To guard him against what she knew was coming. But, astonishingly, she couldn't find the words. They remained frozen in her throat as Ekow exhaled sharply.

'Answer me,' he insisted tightly. 'Is that boy your son? Is there a lover lurking in the background I should know about? *Ewuradze*, are you married?'

Those last words were spat out like poison-coated bullets.

Something sharp lanced between her ribs. He wasn't asking about his son. Ekow wanted to know her relationships status. He was offended that she hadn't informed him who was currently sharing her bed.

'Where do you get off, thinking I owe you that sort of personal information?' she threw at him.

Derisive eyes met hers. 'You know very well why you do. Deny it all you want, but the chemistry that gripped us that night at the bar is still present, and I daresay as potent as ever. Clearly whoever fathered this child—if he's yours—is either no longer in the picture or he's not satisfying you the way someone as passionate as you needs to be satisfied.'

'You're right. On both accounts.'

That all-consuming fire leapt in his eyes again, but before his usual very male satisfaction could shine through he studied her a little more intently. He'd obviously gleaned the deeper meaning to her words.

Again, his gaze swung towards Leo, his incisive gaze sweeping over his chubby features. 'How old is the boy, Eva?' he demanded tersely, and she saw a different tension invading his body.

'He's seven months, three weeks and two days old. And don't insult my intelligence by pretending to make calculations.'

'What…?' He stopped, took a slow, chest-filling breath. He reached out a hand, propping it on the hood of the car. 'What are you saying, Eva? And before you think to toy with me, know that my patience is in serious deficit.'

'I'm saying I got the message loud and clear. My son hasn't been your business since he was conceived. And he's absolutely not your business now.'

A stunning transformation came over his face as he absorbed her meaning. 'What you're saying…that means…'

He staggered one step backwards and it was a sight to behold. Such a pillar of a man seemingly floored by the truth.

Eva wanted to laugh, to mock and dismiss him just

as callously as he'd dismissed her, after she'd spent a sizeable chunk of her precious savings to buy a ticket to Accra to inform him about his impending fatherhood, only to have her efforts thrown back in her face and topped off with threats.

She didn't laugh. Because the reality was nowhere near humorous.

Had he hoped she would temper her words? Perhaps give him a pass so he could deign to acknowledge her somewhere down the line?

She glanced away from him to Leo, the most treasured thing in her life. Jonah, perhaps sensing his impetuousness was causing more ripples than he'd imagined, had stopped in the middle of the lawn and was attempting to calm Leo, who was still holding out his arms, insisting on the love and attention from his mother that was his due.

Unable to deny him, she went over and lifted him into her arms. 'It's okay, my darling. Mommy's here.'

He immediately stopped whimpering, an adorable toothless smile breaking out as he played with the chunky colourful necklace she wore with her dress.

Behind her, Ekow's presence loomed large, and even though he kept his distance she could feel every scrap of his focus fixed on her.

'Give me a proper answer. Now, Eva,' he muttered tersely after a minute had passed.

She shook her head. 'I'm not doing this. Not out here.'

She strode past a wide-eyed Jonah and re-entered her house, achingly aware of Ekow half a step behind.

Yolanda hastily stepped back from the window, and

Eva cringed at the thought that the older woman must have overheard a good chunk of their conversation.

'Is everything okay?' her friend asked.

Before she could answer, Ekow strode into the living room and stopped, his eyes narrowing on her neighbour.

'I need to talk to Eva. Leave us. Please,' he tagged on tersely, his wide-legged stance stating that he wouldn't be moving anywhere anytime soon.

Yolanda's eyes widened, then shifted to Eva, one eyebrow raised in question. Swallowing her irritation at Ekow, as he obliviously tapped out a message on his phone, she smiled at her friend. 'It's fine. Thanks for your help tonight, Yo.'

'No problem.' Her gaze shifted to Jonah, who lingered in the doorway. 'Do you want to come home with me, Jonah? I'm sure Eric wouldn't mind a sleepover,' she said, referring to her son, who was in the same class as Jonah.

For once, her brother looked uncertain, almost contrite as his gaze searched Eva's. 'It's all right. You can go,' she encouraged him.

He gave a nod, rushed to his room, and emerged seconds later with his treasured backpack. Without looking at Ekow, he darted out through the front door.

'I'll call you tomorrow,' Eva said to Yolanda.

'You'd better,' her friend murmured under her breath, her expression rife with curiosity as Eva walked her to the door.

Eva whirled on Ekow as soon as she'd shut the door behind her friend, trying not to dwell on the fact that she was alone with him. 'I'd thank you not to order people about in my home.'

Her words bounced off him, and his broad shoulders lifted in a shrug. 'Feel free to call her back. Let us air our dirty laundry in public, shall we?'

She pursed her lips, seething that he'd called her bluff. 'Let's get this over with,' she said.

But instead of peppering her with the questions brimming in his eyes, he pivoted away from her, putting the width of the small room between them. Then, in a repeat of his stance outside, he leaned forward and gripped the back of the sofa until his knuckles were tight, his bones straining against his dark skin.

For an eternity he stared at Leo, his expression a mixture of shock, awe and bewilderment. 'Is this boy mine?' he finally rasped, his voice like burning gravel.

Something seismic and esoteric shook through her. Perhaps because, despite the callous repudiation she'd suffered at his father's hand, Eva had always held this moment in her heart. Perhaps she'd even placed herself in Leo's shoes, imagined what it would be like to be handed the essential answer to a puzzle, after years of wondering and hoping and yearning over her own father.

'His name is Leo. And you know damn well he's yours. You've known for the better part of a year and a half. So, here's what *I* want to know. Why are you pretending otherwise?'

CHAPTER FOUR

EKOW COULDN'T TAKE his eyes off the child.

He couldn't breathe.

Hell, he was absolutely certain that had he not been gripping the back of the shabby sofa he would've crumpled to the ground.

His child.

His *son*.

One plump cheek was nestled against his mother's chest as he valiantly fought to stay awake and adorably lost the battle. Within a minute, sleep finally overtook him, and his long lashes spread out in half-moon fans. His hair was thick and curly and, courtesy of his mother's mixed heritage, his skin was a soft, dark caramel.

He was...beautiful. Perfect.

Incredible, really, that something so flawless belonged to him.

And he'd had no idea...

Knowing he couldn't disturb the child was the only reason why a torrent of questions stayed locked in Ekow's throat. Why he wasn't bellowing his fury at her outrageous lies.

'He's mine.' Those two words shifted something inside him. Settled a path forward with such clarity that it staggered him all over again.

Ekow had never asked for a role other than the one he'd carved for himself in his dysfunctional family. To make such a demand from the father who'd sired him just to have a son to boast about, and then treated him like an unwanted visitor, would've been as futile and painful as bashing his head against a rock. Far too quickly as a child, he'd learned to rely on no one but himself.

But now he'd been presented with this everything he'd deemed essential faded into insignificance.

Was this…love?

He had no idea. That emotion was alien to him. It had been non-existent in his father. And his mother had been too absorbed in being the perfect wife, too cowed by her overbearing husband, to display any emotion which didn't mirror her spouse's. Perhaps recently, since his father's death, his mother had shown some signs of affection. Unfortunately, any capacity he had to be receptive had been eroded under his father's demanding and cruel boot.

Recently, though, his brother Atu had married. And when Amelie had given birth, shortly after they were married, Atu had been curiously overcome as he'd proclaimed fatherhood as a life-changing experience.

But, while Ekow took his duties as uncle and godfather seriously, his devotion had always felt…removed. He hadn't understood Atu's vow to burn the world to the ground should any harm befall his wife, his daughter, or their baby son.

Right now, in this moment, he knew what his brother

meant. Being confronted with his flesh and blood had already altered the trajectory of his life.

But what he found incomprehensible was that *he hadn't known*.

'All this time you kept me in the dark.' The stark words fell from his lips wreathed in quiet fury and bewilderment. He couldn't shake the thought that he could've gone years, decades, perhaps even his entire life, without knowing his son existed.

And that was unacceptable.

Eva's eyes had widened at the low growl erupting unbidden from his throat. Now she had the audacity to take a step back, as if *he* was the dangerous one here. As if *he* had committed this unconscionable transgression.

She opened her mouth, most likely to spew more lies. But her gaze dropped to the baby. *His baby.*

'I need to put him to bed. We can continue this when I'm done.'

She started to turn away, and a sharp, desperate yearning pierced his heart. 'Wait.'

The word was quiet, but forceful enough to make an impact. She froze.

Ekow dragged in a long, sustaining breath. Released his hold on the weathered sofa. Drew himself up to his full height. On ludicrously shaky legs, he crossed the room to where she cradled the precious bundle who bore his DNA.

He didn't care that the hand he lifted towards his son shook uncontrollably. That another guttural sound rose in his chest as he touched his son's warm, satin-smooth cheek for the first time.

Up close, he was even more beautiful, and his features, now he was examining them closely, bore the un-mistakable Quayson stamp. He didn't need a paternity test to prove this boy was his.

He trailed his hand over his child's silky curls, his tiny shoulders and one tightly furled fist. When it opened to curl around his finger, the sound in his throat erupted in a hoarse, unintelligible sound, unleashing a longing he fought to contain.

Eva's gaze raked his face, and whatever she read there made her nostrils quiver momentarily. Then she gathered herself, sending him another censorious look. He would get to the bottom of that look. Get to the bottom of this whole elaborate ruse of hers to keep what was his from him. Her absurd allegation that he'd known and denied his child's existence.

The reality that he was a father continued to shake through him as he watched her stride down the hall, fighting to stay still when everything inside him clamoured for another glimpse, another touch of his son.

He paced the living room, his unseeing gaze darting over the cheap furniture, the worn carpet and tired curtains.

Evangeline had had his baby, kept it from him, for whatever reason, and chosen to live in a low-income neighbourhood, scraping a living out of a business that was barely breaking even, instead of in the lap of luxury as the mother of his child.

Why?

When she returned ten minutes later, the question erupted out of him.

'Why hide him from me all this time? I could've

given you a much better life than you're living right now. Because money is what all this is about, right?'

She stilled in the small archway framing the hallway. In the reflected light her voluptuous body was thrown into relief, punching fresh lust into the tumultuous emotions churning through him.

'You think this is about *money*?' she spat out with disgust. 'I don't want your money. I never did.'

His mouth twisted. 'You're going to have to do better than that. And why did you imply that I already knew I was a father?'

Her small fists curled. 'It wasn't an implication. It was the truth.'

He shook his head, certain he was hallucinating. 'Do you deny your brother targeted my bank to lure me here?'

For a long second she didn't answer. Then she shrugged. 'No, I don't deny it. But until last night I had no idea what he was doing.'

'You expect me to believe this *truth*, too?' He didn't bother to soften his derision.

An angry flush rushed to her face. 'I don't care what you believe.'

'Yes, you do. At least enough to put on that dress. What were you hoping, Eva? That I would be so bowled over by seeing you in that dress again I'd turn to putty in your hands? Or was it more the memory of my sliding it off your body and indulging in the delights underneath that you hoped would sway me into your way of thinking?'

Her eyes widened. 'What are you—?'

'Because I'll confess it almost worked.'

He confessed that truth tightly. Seeing her when he'd pulled up outside, the dress still clinging in all the right places, had ramped up his temperature to almost lethal proportions.

He'd spent all day debating how best to proceed with Evangeline and her troublesome brother. He'd concluded that the boy didn't belong behind bars. His clearly prodigious talents were better off being nurtured in the right way, under strict supervision.

He'd smugly envisaged how he would convey his magnanimous decision to Eva…perhaps thaw the ice wall she'd erected between them. Hell, he'd even imagined a second performance of their scorching night together—a way to draw a firm line beneath what he still considered unfinished business.

Not for a wild and stunning second had he imagined *this*…

'You think I put on this dress for *you*?' she scoffed.

He ignored his sharp at her tone and raised mocking eyebrows. 'Why else?'

'Did your ego not get out of your way long enough for you to consider that this might be my favourite dress? That I like it, and it's mine, and I can wear it whenever I damn well please? Or do you think the world revolves around your greatness?'

'Look me in the eye and say it didn't once cross your mind.' He modulated his voice in the way that usually confounded his business opponents. His brother had termed it his 'oh, hell' voice.

Ekow favoured it when he wanted to cut through the BS. And, while this issue needed to take a back seat to the more important one of the son he'd been kept in the dark about, he needed to establish a baseline of control. That control included shattering Eva's subterfuge. And what better way to shatter it than to get her to admit her true intentions in wearing the dress?

This time he knew the heat flooding her face wasn't born of fury. It was a live wire of awareness. Perhaps even arousal.

A lethal cocktail of sensations churned through the air, leaving them locked in battle for an eternity before she shook her head. 'This is insane,' she rasped, but he caught the huskiness in her voice, saw the outline of her nipples as she strode forward. 'Do you want to discuss Leo or keep making absurd observations?'

Hearing his son's name sharpened his focus. 'Ah, yes. You insist your brother acted on his own. And that somehow I knew I had a son but denied his existence?'

'Somehow? You know exactly how. Your father was an effective emissary, believe me.'

Every cell in his body froze. 'My *father*? What are you talking about? What has he got to do with this?' he demanded through lips numb with a foreboding he didn't welcome.

She pressed her fingers into her temples before spearing him with another contemptuous look. 'Please, spare me the shocked innocence! I'd say you sent him to do your dirty work, but after meeting him I imagine no one sends your father to do anything. He probably always offers to dispatch another one of your discarded affairs on your behalf. I get it.'

His insides clenched tighter. He felt icier. 'Be careful who you're disparaging, Eva.'

The silky warning drew a sharp inhalation from her,

but to his surprise her chin remained at the defiant angle he'd first seen when he'd watched her toss a drink in her boss's deplorable face.

'You've called me a liar more than once in my own home and now you're warning me about the way *I* treat *you*?'

He slashed a dismissive hand through the air. 'What you're saying never happened. At least own your poor decisions.'

Fire flashed through her eyes and her small, slim hands curled into fists again. 'You don't believe me? Feel free to ask your father.'

He'd thought his insides couldn't get colder, the sensation in his chest more desolate. 'That would be quite impossible since he's no longer alive.'

She stilled, her eyes widening before she swallowed and looked away from him. 'I… I didn't know that. My condolences.'

He stiffened at the gentleness in her voice. It went nowhere towards absolving her of the immutable crime of keeping his son from him.

Almost compelled, he returned his gaze to the door at the end of the hall behind which his handsome son slept. And, yes, he was smug about *that*—because he and Eva had created something beautiful, something extraordinary.

Something he'd been denied.

He opened his mouth but she put up a hand. And, *Yesu*, that regal action was commanding enough to do the job of silencing him—a feat very few people would dare attempt.

'Your father may no longer be in a position to corroborate what I'm saying, but I have proof of my visit.'

His heart hammered and lurched, driving discomfort through his body. Even now, some three decades into the abject knowledge that his father had never favoured him, some part of him still lived in denial.

But if what Eva was saying was true, then his father had...

No.

It was unconscionable to believe his father would've taken such conclusive steps to deny a Quayson the right to claim his own flesh and blood. Or had Ekow been deemed unimportant enough even to run such a conversation past him?

He shook off the dark shadows attempting to pull him deeper into the quiet despair he'd lived with for decades. 'Show it to me,' he said, his voice an alien sound.

Muted hurt flashed across her face. Her lashes swept down and she exhaled slowly, then crossed to the clutch she'd dropped on the coffee table when they'd come indoors.

Ice and dread and fury churned in a lethal cocktail through his gut as he watched her flick through her phone. Her movement was too purposeful to be a bluff, but what else could it be?

Having found whatever she was looking for, she held out her phone. 'See for yourself,' she dared him.

Teeth gritted, he stared down at the screen. At the electronic airline ticket and booking confirmation for a hotel in Accra a handful of weeks after their weekend together.

Ekow couldn't clearly define the sensations shifting through him. He suppressed what felt like relief and reached for cold, hard logic. 'This just shows you travelled to Accra. Your surname is Ghanaian, so I'm assuming at least one of your parents is West African. Your father?'

This time her anguish wasn't muted. It was visceral and thick. And it lasted more than a few seconds. She visibly swallowed before she gathered herself. 'My parentage is none of your business. If you don't believe this, use whatever means you used to track me down. I'm sure there's some footage somewhere that shows I visited the Quayson Hotel in Accra and met with your father exactly when I say I did.'

The churning intensified. Her words were easily verifiable. She wouldn't be so foolish as to risk him calling her bluff. Which meant—

The doorbell sounded, cutting across the unthinkable, unacceptable conclusion his brain wanted to make. He didn't...*couldn't* believe his own father would have done such a thing. Eva had to be lying.

And yet as he trailed her to the door—because he suspected he knew who had rung the bell—he couldn't shake the knot of dread thickening in his gut.

He paused behind her when she opened the door and frowned at the man on the doorstep. 'Can I help you?' she asked.

'He's here for me,' Ekow interjected, then addressed the man. 'Did you do as I asked?'

'Of course, sir.'

Ekow took the bags he held out. 'Thank you, Samson. Return to the hotel. I'll let you know when I need you.'

'Yes, sir. Goodnight, sir.'

Ekow shut the door and found the mother of his son glaring at him.

'What is this? And who was that man?'

'Samson is my driver.' He held up the bags. 'And this isn't quite the meal I intended us to have, but it's dinner, nonetheless. We'll need the fuel, I suspect, since we've barely broached the surface of everything you need to tell me.'

'What *I* need to tell *you*? What makes you think—?'

'Enough, Eva!' He deposited the takeout boxes on her dining table and swivelled to face her. 'We're going to eat, and then you're going to take me through everything that's occurred from the moment you stole out of my bed till now.'

Her chin tilted higher. 'Eat if you must. I've lost my appetite.'

Ekow exhaled long and slow. Had it been anyone else, Eva might have imagined he was at the end of his rope. But then he locked eyes with her and silently reminded her that he was a formidable tycoon who could crush her on a whim.

'My son is seven months old. Are you still breast-feeding him?' he asked, his voice thickening curiously as his gaze dropped to her chest and rose back to her face.

Unwelcome heat engulfing her, she nodded.

'Correct me if I'm wrong, but doesn't that mean you should keep regular eating habits?'

'My eating habits were absolutely fine before you

turned up on my doorstep, Mr Quayson. And my son is perfectly healthy.'

'I'm happy to hear it. Why don't we ensure it stays that way?'

The rigidity edging the question said he wouldn't be moved from his intention. Fighting irritation, and the misguided notion that he cared anything about her, she went into the kitchen to retrieve cutlery and clean plates, telling herself she'd planned to eat with him tonight anyway.

But that was *before* he'd called her integrity into question.

Before he'd looked her in the eyes and called her a liar.

Sure, nothing had changed. Nothing except Ekow Quayson's absurd assertion that he hadn't known his son existed.

She jumped when firm hands closed over her own. 'What are you doing?' she demanded. 'Let me—'

'Your fists are clenched around the cutlery, Eva. I don't want you to hurt yourself,' he said gruffly, calmly prising the utensils from her hands and laying them neatly on the table. 'We haven't reached the blood-shedding part of the evening yet, I don't believe.'

'You think this is funny?'

His face grew granite-hard. 'Believe me, I don't find a single moment of this situation humorous,' he replied, before reaching for the first takeout bag.

Considering the enormity of their situation, it was surreal to watch him laying out the food boxes on the table. It was most definitely the wrong time to recall he'd insisted on feeding her the night they'd met too, as if that aspect of caretaking really was important to him.

Bitterness seared her. Too bad that feeding her was the extent of his nurturing. Too bad that when she'd needed him to show the same level of caring on discovering she was pregnant with his child he'd declined, sending his father to do his dirty bidding...

About to insist he not bother with the food, she held her tongue. Because, for all his arrogance and austere pronouncements, for a fraction of a second Ekow Quayson had seemed...floored by Leo's existence.

There remained a tightness around his eyes, harsh lines bracketing his lips, and the stiff way he held his body looked as if he was bracing himself for something monumental.

For good or ill, she forced herself to consider, for a fraction of a second, if he'd been truly in the dark as he claimed.

'Evangeline.'

His firm, insistent voice said that whatever she believed might not matter. The expressions she'd imagined she'd seen were nowhere in sight when she refocused on him.

He'd pulled out a chair, was waiting for her to take it. Fighting a compulsion she couldn't seem to dismiss, she approached the table. She'd been too riled up to spot the logo on the food boxes before. Now, seeing the veritable feast spread out on her table, she couldn't miss it.

Of course he'd ordered from one of the most exclusive restaurants in Cape Town. She hadn't even known the restaurant did take-out. Perhaps they only did it for powerful billionaires.

She pushed away the nonsensical thought when it threatened to produce a touch of hysteria. If he wanted to throw a layer of civility over this situation she'd go along with it. She mustn't forget Jonah's situation hadn't been resolved either.

So she sat down, striving not to be affected by his proximity, not to inhale the stimulating blend of oak and earth and man pulsing from his skin. Not to watch the hypnotic way he moved when he rounded the table to open the boxes from where the intensely aromatic fragrances emanated.

Eva hated her sudden surge of hunger. The resurgence of the appetite she'd loftily denied.

'You'll have to help me out,' he said stiffly. 'I don't know what nursing mothers are allowed to eat.'

'Unless you're serving fugu, or some super-exotic delicacy, most foods are fine. It's what I drink that I have to watch.'

He nodded curtly, then started to dish out portions with streamlined efficiency. A minute later he set down a plate heaped with mouthwatering linguine and lobster rolled in a creamy sauce, delicate stalks of asparagus, and tapioca chips.

'No pufferfish in sight.'

With that dry delivery, he served himself, then pulled out the adjacent chair.

He ate in silence, his movements precise and unhurried, as if he had all the time in the world. As if the battle they both sensed hovering on the horizon like an impending storm didn't exist.

Determined not to be the first to break the silence,

Eva ate enough to reassure herself that Leo's next feed would be unhindered.

When she placed her cutlery down Ekow's gaze sliced to her half-finished plate, then rose to meet hers. Perhaps her challenge was clear enough. Perhaps he, too, was picking his fights. He set his own tableware down and pierced her with fierce brown eyes.

'When did you find out you were pregnant?' he lobbed at her, his voice tight with bridled emotions.

'A month after I…after we were together. We used protection. I didn't have any reason to think it would fail.'

'Clearly it did. I believe that's what the disclaimer warning on the condom box is for,' he stated in a bone-dry voice.

She stiffened. 'I hope you don't think I helped it along somehow.'

'Did you?' he returned, brooding eyes fixed on her.

'No,' she said, just as coldly. 'You might not believe me, but I detest women who trick men like that.'

'Why wouldn't I believe you?'

His father's harsh words rang in her ears. 'You're a very wealthy man. Isn't that the first conclusion you'd draw? That any woman you sleep with might want to take a nine-month shortcut to wealth and prestige?'

'The women I sleep with know the rules going in. You were an…anomaly.'

'You mean I was a nobody, with no clue to how your sophisticated world works?'

A muscle rippled in his jaw. 'Don't put words in my mouth, Eva. I don't make a habit of picking up women at bars. And I don't think you do the same with men.'

Tight-lipped, she gave a shake of her head.

'So our situation was unique from the start. And I want to know why there's a month's gap between discovering you were pregnant and your arrival in Accra.'

The tension in his voice bewildered her. Then her eyes widened with enlightenment. 'Why? Did you think I was trying to find another solution?'

His shrug was stiff. 'We've agreed our situation was exceptional. If you'd chosen a different path, no one would've been any the wiser.'

'I wanted my baby the second I knew I was pregnant! Leo wasn't planned but he was wanted. Very much.'

He searched her face with such intensity that Eva had to fight not to squirm. Then he nodded, and despite her ruffled emotions something eased inside her.

'It took me two months to reach out to you because I was busy looking for another job. I had bills to pay and a brother to look after. I couldn't just jump on a plane. And you might not be aware of this, but apparently you can't just pick up the phone and ask to speak to the billionaire banker you happened to spend the night with.'

'Two nights,' he returned huskily. 'We spent two nights together.'

Heat spiralled through her as his eyes dropped to her mouth and lingered for far too long. Clearing her throat, she continued. 'When I managed to track you down, I called you. Several times. I didn't get farther than Reception because I refused to give a reason for my call. When I realised only a face-to-face meeting would work, I went to Accra.'

His tension increased, and his eyes were no longer

burning with that all-consuming heat. 'Where you purportedly met my father.'

'Would you like me to describe his office to you? Would that make you believe me or is there some particular reason you're insisting on clinging to the belief that I'm lying?' Something about his heightened tension pushed another possibility at her. 'Or is this something else? Something you don't want to accept because believing me would mean shining a different, unwanted light on the situation?'

Cruel rejection hardened his face. But she sensed she was right. He didn't want to accept her explanation because the alternative was unthinkable.

'You say you met my father. What did he say to you?'

She forced a shrug. 'The usual things men like you say to women like me, I'm guessing. He called my character into question, quizzed me about dates and, like you, claimed I was lying. When I showed him my ultrasound photo he said the child I was carrying could be anyone's.' She took a shallow, non-sustaining breath. 'Then he dismissed me with a threat never to contact you or anyone in your family again.'

She kept her gaze fixed over his shoulder, afraid he'd read every moment of the anguish she'd suffered in her eyes if she looked at him.

His eyes narrowed into vicious slits. 'That's not all. If you're hiding something from me I'll find out. I always do.'

She swallowed her alarm, asking herself why she hadn't mentioned that final thing. 'Is that a threat?'

'No. It's a statement of fact.'

In that moment Eva wanted to scream every brutal word his father had spoken to her in his office. She wanted to jump up, march into her bedroom and retrieve the final act of her humiliation.

The cheque Joseph Quayson had scrawled his signature on and thrown across his desk at her.

Money for her silence. Money so she would never utter his son's name in connection with her *spawn*.

But she'd vowed never to relive those intensely humiliating moments ever again.

She was startled when he surged to his feet, going to the window she'd stared out of only last night as she'd recalled their first meeting. For an age he remained there, a pillar of seething emotions, one hand braced on his nape.

Then he snapped around, his face a hard, determined mask. 'I now know of my son's existence. That's the most important thing here.'

'If that's your roundabout way of saying you don't believe me, be a man and say it.'

Fury flashed across his face. 'You don't want to test me right now, Eva. I want my son. I intend to have him in my life. The only thing I want to discuss now is how to make it happen.'

Alarm shuddered through her. 'You can't just throw down demands and expect me to fall in line.'

A tic appeared at his temple. He shoved his hands into his pockets and rocked back on his heels. 'I've been ignorant of my son's existence for the better part of a year and half so, yes, my speed will be blistering.'

She watched him stride towards her, ferocious intent in every frame of his body.

'You have until morning, Eva. You want me to believe you intended me to be in our son's life from the moment you found out you were pregnant? This is your chance to prove it.'

'By doing what? Interrupting my life and his at your whim?'

If anything, he turned stonier. 'You think this is a whim?'

She swallowed. 'You claim you've only just learned you're a father. Perhaps you should take some time—'

'Absolutely not. He's mine. I'm not denying either myself or him another second without each another.'

Her heart plummeted to her feet. 'What does that mean?'

He dropped his head a little closer to hers, as if he didn't want her to miss his next words. 'It means you and Leo are coming back to Ghana with me.'

Eva reared back, taking several steps away from him. 'What? Are you out of your mind? We're not going anywhere—'

'Do you really want to become embroiled in an international custody battle with me?' he enquired, his voice silky yet deadly. 'Because that wouldn't be my first option, if I were you.'

'You talk about options, but what you're giving me is an ultimatum.'

He shrugged, her accusation bouncing off him. 'Call it what you will. Those are my terms. For you and our son, at least. We're yet to deal with your brother. His situation will require a different plan.'

She felt a dart of shame, because she'd forgotten

about Jonah in the aftermath of Ekow's bombshells. 'What's that supposed to mean? What plan?'

'It means he might need special guidance.'

Her eyes narrowed. 'If that's billionaire-speak for some sort of juvenile detention, be warned that I'll fight you with everything I have!'

One corner of his mouth twisted but the rest of his face remained a tyrannical mask, without an ounce of give. 'Your devotion is admirable. But coddling him isn't the answer, and deep down I think you know it.'

She inhaled sharply. 'He's been through enough.'

'And he's used whatever that was as an excuse to get away with murder. What he needs is structure.'

'And, let me guess, you're going to provide it?' she scoffed, despite a part of her grudgingly accepting that he was right.

He shrugged. 'The level of skill your brother has shown is…exemplary. That kind of genius needs careful harnessing. Agree to my plan and he'll receive the expert guidance he's lacking.'

She knew better than to snatch the carrot he dangled, and yet… 'If I agree, how long do you expect Leo and me to stay in Ghana for?'

'The first few years of his life at the very least. More if we decide he would be better off with us remaining a unit rather than apart.'

Astonishment made her gape for several seconds before she collected herself. 'Excuse me? Did you say the first few *years*? I'm not sure what sort of guests you invite to your home to visit for years, but I don't intend to be one of them.'

Intense eyes rested mockingly on her, and Eva was

sure a snort left his throat before he strolled forward to stand before her.

'You misunderstand, my dear. You're not coming to Accra for a visit. You and our son are coming to live with me. He's going to take my name and his place as my rightful heir. And you, Evangeline, are going to live under my roof as my wife.'

CHAPTER FIVE

SLEEP ON IT.

Those had been Ekow's words before striding out of her house as if he hadn't turned her world upside down.

Her mild hysteria had resurged, ready to break free at the smallest pressure. Perhaps he'd noticed and timed his exit accordingly.

Needless to say, she hadn't slept.

She'd still been staring at the ceiling when Leo had woken up just before sunrise. It had been a relief to leap into the routine of feeding, bathing and setting him up for the day. And she had unashamedly doubled the normal forty-five-minute routine, simply so she could postpone thinking about the seismic change Ekow expected her to make on his say-so.

She'd grasped Yolanda's offer to drive Jonah to school with both hands, had even summoned a smile to put her friend at ease when she'd stopped by to collect Jonah's school things.

Eva knew she'd have to explain herself at some point, but how could she when even *she* didn't know what direction her life was headed?

While Leo contentedly played in his playpen Eva sat at the dining table, cradling a cup of fast-cooling coffee.

She and Ekow had created a son between them, but when it came right down to it, they barely knew each other. While marriage for the sake of their son sounded like a worthwhile sacrifice, was she doing him a disservice by even contemplating it?

Questions continued to tumble through her head.

An hour later, after despatching a client's paperwork, she typed Ekow's name into an online search engine.

After his father's treatment of her in Accra, she'd vowed never to waste another minute on him. But with one click thousands of hits exploded onto the screen.

The Quayson brothers had been deemed supremely eligible bachelors long before the oldest brother had died in a tragic car crash. Now the middle brother, Atu, was married and off the market, Ekow was considered an even more exclusive catch.

Though she knew it was a dangerous path, she couldn't stop herself from reading story after story about his past liaisons, the lengths some of those women had gone to in order to bag a billionaire.

Thirty minutes later, overwhelmed with information, she shut her laptop with more force than necessary, and knotted her hands in her lap as she pursed her lips.

No wonder he'd been sceptical about everything she'd told him. Even just a few minutes in Eva had discovered three separate stories about women who'd tried to lay paternity claims on him.

Rising from the chair with a dash of impatience, she dumped her cold coffee in the sink, then stood frozen, staring at her garden.

Was this why his father had denounced her claim right off the bat? She hadn't given him any evidence, after all. It hadn't even occurred to her that she might need it.

But it didn't excuse his threats and his humiliating her.

Compelled, she went to her bedside table, pulled open the drawer and, after rifling through her documents, pulled out the cheque Joseph Quayson had contemptuously tossed at her that day in his office.

Even after all this time, the zeros on the cheque still boggled her mind.

She should've destroyed it a long time ago. She knew that. She'd questioned herself before and after Leo's birth, but deep down she knew why she hadn't.

It was an effective reminder of her shockingly innocent belief that she was doing the right thing and therefore the father of her child would do the same.

Staring at the cheque, she took comfort in knowing she hadn't let herself be bought off with money. Throughout all her challenges, she'd retained her integrity.

Placing the cheque back in the drawer, she returned resolutely to her laptop.

It had been hard, but she had found the best of all worlds. She got to watch her son grow happy and healthy while building her business from home. She didn't need to change any of it.

Eva let that conviction settle deep inside her as the hours ticked relentlessly towards evening. She was showered and dressed in comfortable clothes, leggings and a light sweater, with Leo propped on her hip and

Jonah tucked away in his room doing his homework, when she answered Ekow's knock.

His laser gaze fastened onto her, conducting a searing head-to-toe scrutiny before swinging to Leo, where it stayed with the same fascination and yearning she'd glimpsed yesterday. Eva released a breath at that look, not even knowing she'd craved this particular reassurance until just now.

Stepping back from the doorway, she let him in. Minutes later she watched his gaze cloud over as she gave him her answer.

'No?'

She wanted to laugh at his incredulous disbelief.

'That's my answer. No, thank you. I won't marry you. What you're offering sounds more like a prison sentence.'

His eyebrows rose. 'A prison sentence? In a prison where your every need is catered for? Where our son will thrive with the best life has to offer?'

Prideful affront hardened her spine. 'You speak as if I'm bringing him up in a gutter.'

He braced his hands on lean hips. 'You're attempting to do your best. I'll give you that. But I'm confident we'll do better together.'

She hated the way he cut her off at the knees, infusing his every argument with statements that made it sound as if he really cared about the son he'd claimed not to know about.

'Why don't you give it a chance?' he pressed.

She couldn't let the lofty dreams she'd had for herself with her own father play out in her son. But then hadn't she scraped together money she could ill afford to buy an airline ticket just so her son would know his father? Was she really prepared to deny him, then put them both through a custody battle she might not win?

Ekow watched steadily, waiting her out, as if simply standing there looking gorgeous and heartrendingly virile would change her mind. After a handful of minutes he slowly sauntered towards her, stopping a foot away.

But he wasn't staring at her.

His gaze was fixed once again on Leo. And it occurred to her that he was seeing him truly awake for the first time. Their son was babbling a mile a minute, his avid gaze swinging between her and his father.

Her heart stopped when he held out one chubby hand to Ekow. Without hesitation, Ekow offered him his hand. Leo eagerly wrapped his fingers around two of his father's and then, to her surprise, started straining towards him.

Ekow's gaze shifted with lightning speed to hers and then returned to fix on his son. 'May I hold him?' The question was gruff, low, infused with feelings and emotions she wasn't quite ready to name.

A lump rising into her throat, she nodded.

Large, secure hands wrapped around Leo's tiny body, and with easy strength Ekow took control of her son.

For a flash in time, panic rose inside her. She understood for the first time that she wasn't in complete control. She'd named Ekow on Leo's birth certificate, which gave him the right to fight for access.

Whether she agreed to marry him or not ultimately didn't matter. He had lawyers, money, power. As much as she loathed to admit it, were she in his shoes she would use whatever she had at her disposal to ensure she was a part of her son's life.

She watched, a bereft feeling widening in her gut, as father and son moved towards the window overlooking the back garden. Ekow murmured low and unintelligible things to his son and Leo answered with enthusiastic babbling.

Part of her wanted Leo to protest, so she could swoop in and reclaim her precious baby, but he simply stared at his father with an avidness that struck her in the chest. Leo might be too young to comprehend his connection with the man holding him, but that would change very quickly.

Would he blame her for the path she was choosing just as she'd secretly blamed her mother for the choices she'd made?

The weight of her decision dropped on her, shaking through her as Ekow pivoted and slowly retraced his steps back to her.

When he stopped in front of her he didn't hand Leo back. In fact, his arms seemed to have been made to cradle his son, and she felt his ease with Leo striking her deep inside. She recalled that Atu's wife had young children, making Ekow an uncle. A few thousand miles away there was an extended family her son didn't know yet.

Deep in her bones she knew Ekow wouldn't give up his son, regardless of the answer she'd just given him.

'Do you know what I did this afternoon?' he asked.

His casual question threw her. 'No,' she answered warily.

'I visited Jonah's school.'

Anger sparked to life inside her. 'You did what?'

A smile quirked one corner of his mouth. 'I wanted to see the environment he was being educated in.'

'You had no right,' she replied hotly.

'Take it easy. I didn't interrupt his studies or ask to see his school records. What I did was assess things for myself. Do you want to know my conclusion?'

She pursed her lips and didn't answer. She knew what he was doing. What she'd been attempting to do herself but hadn't so far because of her financial constraints. Because scholarships for the kind of school Jonah needed were like gold dust.

Ekow answered anyway. 'Your brother is wasted in that place. I think you know it.'

'You seem to think you have all the answers.'

'I do,' he delivered arrogantly. 'I spoke to the heads of two schools renowned for their nurturing of prodigious talents like Jonah's. With the right incentives, both are prepared to take him immediately.'

Eva gasped. 'What gives you the right to make decisions about Jonah without consulting me?'

'No decision has been made yet. But if you think I'm going to sit around twiddling my thumbs while you make up your mind one way or the other, you're wrong.'

'You think packing my brother off to some school is going to make me fall in line with what you want?'

'No. For starters we won't be doing anything your brother doesn't want for himself.'

She frowned. 'What's that supposed to mean?'

'I told you I'd researched him before I arrived here. Part of that research showed me where his interests lie.

He probably hasn't told you about it because he knows there are stumbling blocks in the way of what he wants.'

'And you think you know what Jonah wants?'

He smiled, and while it wasn't cruel, it wasn't kind either. 'Did you know he wants to attend a boarding school in Switzerland? A school especially renowned for harnessing Silicon Valley prodigies?'

Her guilt intensified, and her gaze strayed down the hallway to her brother's closed door.

'His second choice is an equally excellent choice, right here in South Africa. The third choice is in Dubai. I know you've applied for scholarships and been refused on the Dubai school. I can make all three accept him. Just say the word.'

'Really? You would…?' She stopped herself from snatching at his offer. Reminded herself that it came at a price.

'Yes. I would,' he confirmed anyway.

His utter confidence shook through her. With a click of his fingers he could change her brother's life.

'All of this is conditional, isn't it?' she said.

'Of course it is,' he stated briskly, as if she were a little bit slow. 'You care about your brother. He needs more help than you're able to provide him right now. The quicker you face that, the quicker we can get on to more pressing matters.'

'You mean like you not taking no for an answer?'

He looked down at Leo for a long moment before lifting his head. 'He's mine. I won't leave him behind. With your brother where he needs to be, you'll have one less thing to worry about.'

'And you don't get that one of the other things I

worry about is you?' Eva immediately cringed at the telling phrase. When his eyes narrowed, she knew she'd given herself away. Yes, she was afraid of giving in to him. As much as she wanted to deny it, that live wire of sexual chemistry was alive and kicking between them. The more she remained in his orbit, the weaker her defenceless grew.

'State your concerns and I'll be happy to address them.'

Eva wrapped her arms around herself, as if that would stop the unwanted zings from firing through her system. She needed to concentrate on a more grounded argument for not wanting to go ahead with this.

I won't leave him behind.

His words echoed through her brain, growing louder by the second.

She didn't need debate to know he meant every word. 'We could live together, without marriage, for a year or two.'

The words tumbled out of her mouth before her brain recognised what she was saying. But it didn't matter because he was already shaking his head.

'No. I want my son secure and untroubled for his formative years at the very least. He needs stability and I intend to give him that. It's marriage or nothing, Evangeline.'

'What if we can't stand each other?' she threw out wildly, attempting to ignore the way her heart leapt. 'What if we start this absurd union and end up at each other's throats within months?'

As if he couldn't help himself, he returned his gaze to Leo. For an age, he remained silent, and then, 'For our son's sake, I'll attempt to curb whatever habits you find unacceptable. I'll even accommodate whatever characteristics you possess that you think are demonic enough to drive me away,' he said wryly.

'Just like that?'

His gaze raced up then, to spear hers in an intractable hold. 'Do you not think he's worth it?' he asked.

For the second time Ekow had cut her off at the knees. Because the answer was so clear, so inexorable, she could only reply one way. 'Yes, he is.'

Triumph blazed in his eyes and he gave a brisk nod. 'So we're agreed. We will marry.'

It wasn't a question. It was a statement of undertaking that he expected her to agree to.

The foundations of her world shook. She'd all but agreed to hand over her life to him for the foreseeable future. To uproot her life for the son she loved.

'For our son's sake. For Jonah's sake,' Ekow's deep voice compelled, sensing her wavering.

But was she forgetting herself in all of this? Somewhere in all the parenthood books she'd read whilst pregnant with Leo there had been an insistence on self-care. She would turn her life inside out for Leo, but wasn't *she* also worth a little consideration? What exactly would marriage to a dynamic billionaire entail for her? Despite his father having passed away, how was she to know how other members of his family would treat her?

'Evangeline…'

There was a dangerous pitch to his voice, demanding an answer. But it was hard for her to accept what he was offering.

She shook her head. 'Marriage for an undefined time is a…a big undertaking.' His nostrils flared, but before he could open his mouth she continued. 'You've set out your conditions. I have some of my own.'

'Let's hear them,' he growled.

The first searing objection was one she didn't want to voice. It would give her away. Would lay bare the path of her thoughts. But Eva decided she couldn't *not* speak it. 'I don't want… I think it would be best if we live in separate residences.'

His eyes narrowed. 'Excuse me?' His voice positively sizzled with displeasure.

'For the sake of propriety.'

'You must have missed the part where I said you would be staying under my roof.'

His scornful tone shuddered through her. But she held her ground. Lifted her chin. 'I won't be sleeping with you. And the last thing I want is for us to be in a position where we have to tolerate each other's… activities.'

His face clenched into an icy mask. 'You intend to have lovers whilst married to me?'

'No,' she protested hotly. 'But I assumed… I thought… I don't know what to think. About you.'

'What exactly does that mean?'

She shrugged. 'You're a man. With needs. I'm not foolish enough to think that you have plans of remaining celibate for however long we're married.'

His lips twisted. 'How very stoic of you to embrace nun-hood while labelling me a Lothario.'

'Am I wrong?' she demanded, a touch desperately.

His jaw clenched. 'Yes. And make no mistake. There

will be no lovers for you or for me. You're wrong if you think either of us will last a month without giving in to what comes naturally. But I'm willing to wait you out.'

Heat climbed into her face, then rushed in the opposite direction to pool low in her belly. 'You'll be waiting a very long time,' she stated, with more confidence than she felt.

His languid gaze slid over her, conducting a slow, torturous journey from her head to foot and back again to settle on her mouth. 'We'll see. And to return to your suggestion—no. There will be no separate residences. You'll live in my house, sleep in my bed. To our son and to every member of our families this marriage will appear real. Only the two of us will know the truth.'

He was a formidable man to face down, but she was no shrinking violet. She had no intention of sharing his bed again, of giving her body to him.

Once—with her being a virgin—it had been an earth-shaking experience, after which her life had altered irreparably. Now, within twenty-four hours of him resurfacing, he'd set it on a different course entirely. Again. Giving him more ground, losing control around him, was a sure-fire way to invite disaster.

'Are we agreed, Evangeline?'

She took a deep breath. Everything was blurring around her but the figure of father and son standing before her. That was the image she needed to hold in her mind. She was doing this for Leo. Giving him the stability, the love, the freedom of growing up without the question marks she been unlucky enough to have. She needed to hold that as her divining rod. And the bonus was that Jonah would receive the advantages he deserved.

So why did it feel as if she was pulling out her own soul? As if she was pushing her son and her brother into the light while she left herself in the dark?

It didn't matter, she thought impatiently. The sacrifice would be worth it.

Ekow took another step closer, placing himself within touching distance. Whether it was deliberate or not, it reawakened cravings she didn't want to have. From the moment she'd set eyes on him she'd known he was temptation she should resist. She hadn't been able to resist then, and every second in his presence now was a battle with that temptation.

The compulsion to breathe him in assailed her. She took a deep breath, felt the evocative scent of man and aftershave wind itself inside her, dredging up torrid memories she needed to deny, but couldn't.

It was time to answer him.

She forced herself to meet his gaze, to hold it as the earth beneath her feet shifted once more. 'Yes. I'll marry you.'

His jaw clenched tight once. His slow exhalation reeked of triumph. But of course he wasn't done. 'The rest, Eva. Let's hear it, so there's no misunderstanding between us,' he commanded.

'I will live under your roof. But I won't sleep in your bed. That is my offer. Take it or leave it. Give your family whatever excuse you need to, but it won't happen.'

For another long spell he simply stared at her. Then he shrugged. 'Accepted. We'll marry within the month.'

Shock spiralled through her. 'What?'

She wasn't sure whether to be upset at how easily he'd accepted the 'no sleeping together' clause, as if it didn't matter, or to be glad he hadn't argued the point. But, more than that, the idea of disassembling her life in a matter of weeks triggered panic.

'I can't marry you in one month.'

'Why the hell not?' he growled.

'Because I have obligations here in Cape Town. Clients. And Jonah has school.'

'We'll inform the school he'll be leaving immediately. If you agree, of course. I think it's best we get him into one of the other schools as soon as possible, don't you?'

She bit her lip. He was right, but she was reluctant to admit it. 'I'll talk to him.'

He glanced down the hall and raised an eyebrow, clearly expecting her to fall in line again. Before she could answer one way or the other the door to Jonah's bedroom opened and he walked out, freezing when they turned to face him.

'What?'

She approached him, nerves eating at her. 'Come in. I have some news.'

She'd expected him to object, to throw Ekow more of those hostile looks he'd subjected him to yesterday. But with each word she spoke his eyes widened, and when she was done he gave a short, shocked laugh.

'Are you serious? I get to go to that awesome school in Switzerland?'

'If that's your preference, yes,' Ekow said. 'With some conditions, of course.'

Again, she expected Jonah to protest, but he just nodded. 'Yeah, sure. Whatever.'

Eva's eyes widened. 'You're not upset about leaving here? Leaving home?'

His gaze met hers. 'That's the best school in the world for computing, sis. And Cape Town...' He shrugged again. 'It reminds me too much of Mum. I think we both need to move on from all that...don't you?' he mumbled.

Tears prickled her eyes. She tried to speak around the lump in the throat. When she failed, she merely nodded.

He turned back to Ekow. 'Do you mean it? You're not just going to ghost Leo and Eva again, are you?'

'I hardly...' Ekow cleared his throat. 'I mean it,' he confirmed. 'But I need reassurance from you as well. If you step out of line there will be consequences.'

A long, steady look passed between the man she'd agreed to marry and her brother. Then Jonah nodded. At Ekow's echoing nod, her brother turned and grinned at her.

It struck her then that it had been a while since she'd seen a true smile from him. It grated a little that Ekow was the reason for it, but she smothered the feeling.

'Okay, can I go now?'

At her nod, Jonah strolled to the fridge and grabbed a bottle of fizzy soda before disappearing back to his room.

When they were alone again, Ekow's eyes locked on hers. 'Say it again, Eva.'

She took a deep breath. 'I'll marry you.'

CHAPTER SIX

Two weeks later

EVANGELINE MADE TWO discoveries in the fortnight following her agreement to become Ekow Quayson's wife.

One, that money and power ruled the world. Or, in her case, whether a wedding was staged for convenience or whether it was between two people head over heels for each other, it didn't change the juggernaut of over-the-top planning, over-the-top lavishness, and a determination to make it the most talked-about wedding of the decade once that intention was birthed. In fact, it took on a life of its own, and it was impossible to stop it.

Two, that somewhere along the line she'd buried any desire or dreams of a fairy tale wedding with a floaty white dress, a tasteful tiara and a veil. Had shoved away any fantasies of giggling bridesmaids and a champagne-fuelled, dancing-in-a-limo hen night, followed by a luxury spa day, in favour of cold, hard reality.

Years of watching her mother struggle and fall sick, years of caring for her while ensuring Jonah was safe and healthy, had eroded all fanciful thoughts of happy-ever-after. She'd stoically carved a different vision for herself. One which didn't include a laundry list of what she wanted for her own purportedly dream wedding.

And even faced with unrelenting reality and a future mother-in-law with an unlimited budget, Evangeline discovered she still couldn't summon up enthusiasm for her wedding. Because it was a *sham*.

Which brought her to the third problem. Her lack of enthusiasm didn't thrill her future husband or mother-in-law.

It had started with a strained conversation when Ekow had briskly informed her that the guest list had topped a thousand.

Her shocked laughter at the number had elicited a clenched-jaw reaction, and their conversation must've reached his mother too, because Evangeline had been informed stiffly over breakfast the next morning that the list had been trimmed to an immovable seven hundred and fifty.

Evangeline's flippant shrug hadn't gone down well.

Naana Quayson had left the breakfast table with an affronted sniff to seek the company of her new grandson, while Ekow had levelled a narrow-eyed stare at her before refocusing on the *Financial Times* he was reading.

Evangeline had returned to her Iberian ham, boiled egg and toast, stoically chewing before washing it down with coffee.

And if the stiffness between them hadn't yet dissipated… Well, she blamed everything on the speed with which her life had been turned inside out. The faster she tried to acclimatise to her new life the more surreal it seemed.

Hell, most mornings she expected to open her eyes and find herself back in her old bed in Cape Town, staring at the faint brown rain stains on the ceiling, not tucked away in the master suite of a grand mansion sitting over a small hill in the gated enclave known as Quayson Hills.

Within two days of arrival she'd discovered that the prime real estate within the ultra-exclusive location was mostly inhabited by a Quayson uncle, third cousin or great-aunt. She literally couldn't walk down the street without bumping into someone connected by blood to her future husband.

Besides the Quayson clan, only the very *crème de la crème* of the highest social echelon were invited to live within the enclave. Each jaw-dropping mansion was more stunning than the last, but of course Quayson House, holding pride of place atop its own hill, further shattered any illusions that this was going to be in any way a 'normal' if convenient marriage.

If there were two bright spots to be celebrated in the organised chaos that had ensued once she'd stepped off the private jet at Kotoka International Airport, one was that Leo had been accepted wholeheartedly into the Quayson clan. Her baby couldn't be more loved if she'd made a wish upon a thousand stars and had every one of them come true. And the other was that Jonah was ensconced in his new boarding school in Switzerland and already loving it.

Did it break her heart a little that she'd gone from seeing him every day to talking to him only a hand-ful of times on the phone? Yes. But she'd forced herself to see the big picture. At least where her brother was concerned.

More and more, though, she was wondering why a wedding was even necessary, considering Leo's rousing acceptance by the Quayson family...

Which was far less than *she* had received.

Where her son had been gushed over, Evangeline had been met with a tight-lipped coolness and daring probes as to which Annan family she hailed from.

Her evasiveness hadn't earned her any brownie points. But then how could she tell them she didn't know? That their assumption of her surname being her father's was wrong? How could she say that her mother had given both her children her name because she'd never married and had refused to divulge any details of the men who had fathered her children? That she had very little to no knowledge of her Ghanaian heritage because her mother had made South Africa her home and proceeded to forget all about her birthplace?

It was none of their business, Evangeline had assured herself. But somewhere deep inside the cold knot of loneliness had tightened. Along with the shame, the dejection and rejection. She couldn't proudly say she hailed from the royalty-adjacent Saltpond Annans, or the renowned Cape Coast Annans, or even the Takoradi Annans, because her mother had refused to talk about her family.

It didn't matter, she'd stressed to herself, after yet another mild probing over arrangements for the traditional 'knocking' ceremony.

Ekow's mother's new desire to stretch out the nuptials for several weeks was what had finally roused

Treat Yourself to Free Books and Free Gifts.

Answer 4 fun questions and get rewarded.

We love to connect with our readers! Please tell us a little about you...

	YES	NO
1. I LOVE reading a good book.		
2. I indulge and "treat" myself often.		
3. I love getting FREE things.		
4. Reading is one of my favorite activities.		

TREAT YOURSELF • Pick your 2 Free Books...

Yes! Please send me my Free Books from each series I select and Free Mystery Gifts. I understand that I am under no obligation to buy anything, as explained on the back of this card.

Which do you prefer?

❏ **Harlequin Desire®** 225/326 HDL GRAN
❏ **Harlequin Presents® Larger-Print** 176/376 HDL GRAN
❏ **Try Both** 225/326 & 176/376 HDL GRAY

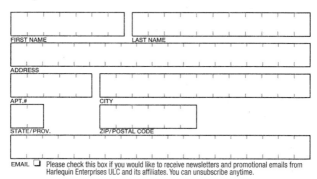

FIRST NAME   LAST NAME

ADDRESS

APT.#   CITY

STATE/PROV.   ZIP/POSTAL CODE

EMAIL ❏ Please check this box if you would like to receive newsletters and promotional emails from Harlequin Enterprises ULC and its affiliates. You can unsubscribe anytime.

HD/HP-520-TY22

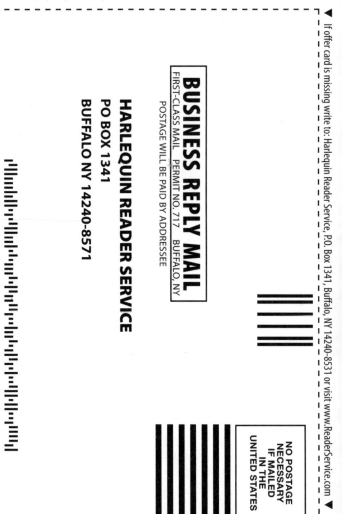

HARLEQUIN Reader Service **—Here's how it works:**

Evangeline enough to hunt down her future husband, three Saturdays after her arrival. Thinking she'd have to call or text to have a conversation with him, since he worked long hours at his bank even at the weekends, she'd been stunned when the house staff had directed her outside.

Evangeline had found him lounging beside the immense swimming pool, with the son she'd thought was still taking his early-afternoon nap busy exploring a selection of the wonderful new toys his father and his many relatives had showered him with. Evangeline couldn't take more than a few steps in the immense house without tripping over yet another gift delivered by a family relation or a friend with an impressive pedigree.

Her child—the newly discovered Quayson—had become something of a celebrity.

'I didn't know Leo was awake,' she'd said.

She hadn't meant it to sound like an accusation, but the notion that she hadn't known the whereabouts of her own child had rubbed her the wrong way, despite Leo looking exceedingly content, sitting on a fluffy blanket surrounded by protective cushions, with wide umbrellas shading his delicate skin from the harsh sun.

Ekow had lifted his gaze from where it had been fixed on his son. Although his eyes had been shielded by a pair of designer shades, she'd known he was staring at her because her skin had grown hot, awareness shooting through her like low-level fireworks.

'I was nearby when he woke up. I asked the staff not to disturb you.'

'It's not a disturbance to look after my own son.' This time the bite in her tone had been undisguised.

Leo had looked up from the bright orange toy he was rattling and beamed at her. His unabashed joy had calmed her roiling senses.

Ekow's nostrils had flared slightly before he'd surged upright. 'Accepted. But you should work your way into being okay with me spending time with my son without your express permission, Eva,' he'd said.

Her heart had thumped hard once, and the feeling of not being in control any more had swelled inside her. 'I thought he was sleeping. I wasn't expecting to find him awake and out here with you.'

'So you were looking for me?'

The barest hint of smugness in his tone had made her hands curl.

'Maybe now you're reassured our son's fine, you can sit down and can tell me why you were looking for me when I understand there are wedding matters for you to discuss with my mother. Albeit reluctantly, I'm told.'

She had paused, bristling at this indication that his mother had discussed her with him. Then, 'That's what I want to talk to you about.'

Not missing her clear irritation, he'd plucked off his sunglasses and speared her with narrowed eyes as she'd taken the lounger next to him. Then wished she hadn't when she'd become acutely aware of the powerful play of muscle in his hair-dusted thighs, the impressive outline of his manhood barely disguised by the swim shorts, and his far too mouth-watering torso so close she could have reached out and stroked his warm skin.

Her gaze had fallen on the strong arms braced on his

knees and she'd fought to ignore the stronger fireworks shooting off inside her.

'You *could* drum up some enthusiasm for your own wedding,' he'd stated, a touch of chill in his tone.

Evangeline had aimed her gaze at a spot on the curve between his neck and shoulder, hoping it would be less disrupting to her senses, only to recall how it had felt to bury her face in that very spot, sinking her teeth into his firm skin as he surged deep and hard and utterly blissfully inside her.

Focus!

'It's difficult to conjure up enthusiasm for several hundred people I've never met before,' she'd replied.

'My mother invited you to make a list of your own, I believe.'

The smile she had attempted in the name of civility had felt dry and tight. 'And I told her it wasn't necessary.'

He'd studied her for a few more seconds. 'You know that only invites more questions, don't you? Especially with someone as inquisitive as my mother?'

Evangeline *had* noticed that the mistress of the house positively thrived on knowing everyone's business. Her attachment to the smartphone which trilled and pinged with endless phone calls and text messages easily rivalled Jonah's attachment to his electronic gadgets.

'Does it matter who I do or don't invite? You've got what you wanted. You've secured your son as you wished.'

When he had remained thin-lipped and displeased, she'd continued.

'It's not too late to change your mind, you know.'

Why her insides had quivered as she'd spoken those words she'd refused to examine. 'We can call this off, come to a new arrangement—'

'No. There will be no calling it off. You've gone to great lengths to assure me that you're going a certain way, that your word is to be believed. Don't try and go another way now or you'll disappoint us both. Our agreement stands. And that includes the part where you strive to act as if this marriage is real. I may not care what people think generally, but I'd rather not be forced to deny that you're doing this wholly against your will,' he delivered acerbically.

That had been yesterday.

He'd invited her to join him and their son there at the pool, albeit with a cool voice and even cooler eyes. But the invitation had been tested immediately when another house staff member had stepped out to inform her she was needed by the wedding planner.

Ekow had stared at her with one eyebrow raised.

She'd stiffly declined his invitation.

And the well-oiled wheels of their wedding plans had continued to spin.

The grounds of Quayson House had been transformed, and despite her determination to remain grounded, untouched and removed, a small corner of Evangeline's heart had been affected by the magic being created around her.

On one side of the estate white pavilions had been erected by expert craftsmen, and a processional path had been created, leading to a large platform upon which she'd stand and make her vows to Ekow.

On the other side, the more traditional set-up for the morning 'knocking' ceremony before the afternoon wedding was also taking shape.

But the last thing she could afford was to be sucked into it.

She'd effectively given up years of her life for her son's happiness. While she would have given her very life for him, didn't she deserve to retain her sanity, her soul, her heart for herself? Didn't she need to safeguard herself from the husband and the family who had already judged her and found her lacking?

Now she stood on top of a small round dais set up in her room by the wedding gown designer. And again she felt that touch of magic she knew she should resist. Because the dress seemed plucked from a discarded dream—a fantasy she'd dismissed before she'd grown out of playdates and tutus.

Tasteful, demure but stylish, it was a perfect medley of lace and silk, with delicately embroidered butterflies stitched into the lightest chiffon neckline, long sleeves, and a waterfall train that sprang from a slit at the back of the pencil skirt.

While full skirts and elaborate trains on wedding dresses had their place, they weren't for her. This classy design, with its equally unfussy veil hanging from a simple diamond-encrusted hair comb, suited her perfectly.

'This one,' she muttered.

The designer exchanged startled looks with the wedding co-ordinator. 'Do you want to try any of the others? We have two dozen more…*classic* gowns for you to—'

'This one,' she said more firmly. If she had to find

a little bit of enjoyment through this ordeal, she'd find it in this.

Matching shoes were presented for her to choose from. She was in the middle of selecting a kitten-heeled satin pair when Ekow's mother walked in.

She had a presence that rivalled her son's. Despite her advancing years, her dark mahogany skin glowed with vitality and her greying hair was styled with such expertise it was difficult to imagine her not wearing the same style in her youth. The few lines around her eyes and mouth were mitigated by light, delicate make-up, and on her tall, slim frame she wore a soft purple kaftan with a stunning embroidered detail that drew the eye to the dark gold necklace gracing her throat.

Eyes the same shade as Ekow's glanced around her as she stopped in the middle of the room. 'How are we getting on? Have we tried any dresses on yet?'

Eva gritted her teeth when she directed the question to the staff instead of her.

'A choice has been made, Mrs Quayson,' the designer said, pointing to the gown Evangeline had chosen.

Naana Quayson's eyes widened, before her face darkened with a frown. 'This? I don't remember this being in the selection.'

'Your son added two dresses this morning,' the designer said. 'This is one of them.'

Evangeline gasped softly.

Ekow had chosen her gown.

Just as she hadn't spent time imagining a fairy tale wedding, she hadn't expended any energy on silly wedding traditions. She didn't mind that he'd seen the dress before she walked down the aisle. But she did mind that he might read something into her choosing one of the dresses he'd selected.

How had he even known?

'I'm not sure where he got the idea to add those. They don't make any sort of statement. No, I don't think that one would be suitable at—'

'I like the dress,' Eva interjected. 'That's my choice.'

'How can you know without trying any of the others?' Naana replied haughtily.

'I know,' Eva insisted. 'And I'm sure there are things we can be doing other than wasting an hour or two on gowns when I've already made up my mind?'

Silence descended in the room.

'At least you're taking an interest, finally,' Naana said after several seconds, her tone starchy with disapproval. 'If you're sure that's the dress you want, we'll move on. Do you feel up to picking a bouquet arrangement?'

She didn't, but with Ekow's admonition echoing in her head she had no choice but to nod. 'Of course. Lead the way.'

Three nights later, in bed after another hectic day of wedding activities, Eva admitted that perhaps getting involved wasn't so bad. That she might even grow to like some of the Ghanaian traditions her mother had told her about, and others she'd discovered on her own.

Since Eva had no older relatives of her own, Ekow's brother had offered to stand in as her representative for the knocking ceremony—a process that involved a representative member of her fiancé's family literally knocking on her family's door and asking to be allowed in to seek her hand in marriage. Using a Quayson shouldn't have been allowed, since it was essentially a conflict of interest, but it seemed both brothers were happy to flout tradition for the sake of marrying the women they'd chosen.

She'd smiled and chuckled in all the right places, but had stopped herself from correcting the mistaken assumption that Ekow had allowed this because he desired her, when Atu's wife, Amelie, had amusingly retold the story of how her husband had gate-crashed her own knocking ceremony and asked for her hand in marriage when, traditionally, it was left to the elders of the family to do so.

The reminder that she'd agreed to this marriage appearing real had echoed at the back of Eva's mind during the afternoon tea her future sister-in-law had arranged for them, and she'd mostly smiled as the young, beautiful and self-assured woman had relayed anecdotes about her own wedding.

Eva had felt a little ashamed for her pang of jealousy at seeing Atu and Amelie so evidently in love, and had instead dwelt on their mutual adoration of their daughter Amaya and young son, Kobi.

That was an emotion she knew well, echoing her cherished feeling for her own son. A feeling she was sure Ekow too shared, if his apparently complete obsession with Leo was any testament.

Their marriage would be another matter entirely, of course…

Leo's distressed cry pulled her out of her rumination, and away from the even more dangerous thought that she might not mind her wedding ceremony after all. Might even relax her guard for a few hours and attempt to enjoy it…

Another cry launched her out of bed.

The nursery adjoined her suite, a vast space she was fairly sure was bigger than her entire Cape Town house. Crossing the room, she suppressed the frisson of worry feathering over her skin. Leo was a good baby. He'd started sleeping almost through the night a few weeks ago. Now, at just past midnight, he should've been fast asleep. But when she reached him his face was creased in misery and his plump arms and legs were punching the air in unhappiness.

'Hey, sweetheart. Hush…' she crooned as she lifted him and cradled him close.

'What's wrong?'

The question was gruff and tight.

She spun to find Ekow framed in the doorway, a frown clenched between his brows. A pair of silk pyjama bottoms rode low on his hips and she quickly averted her gaze before he caught her gaping at his topless perfection.

'What are you doing up?' she asked, then cringed at the inane comment.

'I wasn't asleep. I heard him crying through the monitor.'

Of course he had a monitor in his bedroom. Just as he'd had baby carriers installed in all the vehicles in his fleet of that weren't sports cars. His level of devotion was admirable. And yet she couldn't help her lingering anxiety.

Her breath snagged in her throat as he prowled towards them, his gaze on fixed his whimpering, squirming son. Telling herself she didn't want him to look at her at all, she watched him smooth a long, gentle finger down Leo's cheek.

'What's up, champ?' he asked, his voice low and rumbling.

His scent hit her nostrils when she finally took a breath, and it was all she could do not to groan at the delicious, decadent scent of earth and spice.

'I think he's teething,' she offered, desperate to focus on Leo, to strengthen the walls of her crumbling resistance against his father.

Of course her suggestion swiftly redirected Ekow's focus to her. Her gaze met his a second before his eyes lanced over her, immediately drawing her attention to the thin, short nightdress she wore. And the tiny thong she wore beneath it.

Eva barely heard him when he said, 'He's the right age for that.' But she couldn't hold back her surprise.

'You know what age he should be teething?'

A wry, tense smile whispered over his lips before disappearing. 'I've missed enough of my son's life. I'm determined I won't miss any more.'

She wasn't sure whether there was blame in his tone or whether the chill of his words was directed at something…someone else. But needing to focus on Leo, she chose to let it go.

'What can I do?' he said, after another tense moment had passed.

Again, she suppressed her astonishment. But she had no yardstick to judge this initial phase of fatherhood by, did she? She didn't know if this was the obsession before indifference, or if Ekow truly intended to be invested in every aspect of his son's life.

She nodded towards the bathroom. 'There's some teething powder in the cabinet. If you don't mind...?'

He was already striding across the room.

Rather than stand there gaping at the hypnotic ripple of muscle in his back as he moved, she headed for the rocking chair set beneath a window overlooking the garden. Perching on it, she bounced Leo on her knees. But his agitation merely increased, and one small fist was wedged between his tiny lips as he tried to alleviate his distress.

Ekow returned with the medication and crouched in front of them. 'May I?'

It was as if a large rock blocked Eva's throat at the gruff question. Pressing her lips together, she nodded haltingly, reminding herself again that it had only been a few weeks. True fatherhood meant holding on when things got tough. It meant going the distance through thick or thin. And yet watching Ekow gently tending to their son made a peculiar knot melt inside her.

It was almost a relief when Leo protested loudly again. It meant she could direct her focus to him. Not wonder at the depths of Ekow's emotions. Not wonder if he would even make the first year of their agreement. If she and Leo would find themselves on their own sooner rather than later, like her mother had.

'Evangeline?'

His steady focus and firm tone said he'd been trying to get her attention for a while. Clearing her throat, she flicked a glance at him. Nope. His proximity was still an issue, with that maddening slope of neck into shoulder making her fingers itch to caress the spot.

'Hmm?'

'I asked if you had any other ideas?'

She nodded briskly. 'Yes.'

Without elaborating further, she repositioned Leo and started to lower one spaghetti strap of her nightdress. Then nerves hit her. Her hips had thickened during pregnancy, and her breasts had also grown larger. Elsewhere on her body, a few veins and stretch marks charted the path of her pregnancy.

'It's a natural act. You don't need to be shy around me.'

Despite the heat invading her system, she shrugged. 'I'm not.'

His gaze dropped to her chest, and the charged look that triggered this insane chemical reaction between them sparked to life.

'Do you want me to leave?' he asked, his voice even thicker than before.

Perhaps she was foolish to be pleased by her effect on him. Because surely she was either playing with fire or inviting a situation she would regret later? But she mildly stunned herself by slowly shaking her head.

'No, you don't need to leave.'

Then she lowered her strap.

Supremely conscious of Ekow's eyes on her as she fed Leo, it was a miracle that she managed not to squirm. Or revel in the heady sensation his undiluted attention triggered in her.

CHAPTER SEVEN

He didn't take his eyes off her even when Leo kicked out one foot. Ekow caught it, and the sight of her son's small foot in his father's large palm threatened to dissolve that knot inside her completely.

To alleviate the feeling, she bent low and dropped a kiss on her baby's head.

'He's beautiful,' Ekow said, a note of quiet awe in his voice.

'I'm a little terrified he's going to get egotistical with the amount of compliments showered on him these past weeks.'

Ekow nodded gravely. 'I can see how that might become a problem. We'll ensure it's limited to just one compliment a day, then.'

For some absurd reason Eva had the maddest urge to smile—to laugh, even. 'Yes, I think that would suffice.'

One corner of his mouth quirked, and she was fiercely reminded of the night they'd met. Of their easy conversation over dinner while deep and turbulent undercurrents of sexual promise had meandered between them. He'd literally charmed the clothes off her body, and she'd been more than willing to let him.

Before she could be drawn deeper into memory's dangerous quagmire, Leo lost interest in being fed and gave another wail. Straightening her nightie, she bounced him against her shoulder. But after five minutes with no success in calming him Ekow glanced at her.

'We should take him for a drive. I've heard it's a good way to help agitated babies sleep.'

She nodded. 'It works. I've done it a few times when he wouldn't settle.'

One eyebrow cocked sardonically. 'In that rust bucket you called a car?'

She lamented the demise of the car Ekow's people had disposed of, along with whatever else she'd left behind in Cape Town, but she lifted her chin. 'She served me well. And I won't have a bad word said against her.'

He stood, held up his hands in mock surrender and took a melodramatic step back. Eva wanted to smile again. She disguised the urge by burying her face in her son's neck—a move that was rewarded with another irritated cry.

'I'll get dressed,' Ekow said, pivoting on his heel to return to his suite.

For a moment she sat there, wondering if it was too late to salvage the foolish melting sensation in her belly. Wondering how quickly she could kill the fizz starting inside her at the thought of taking a drive with Ekow. At the thought of being alone with him after the mad circus she'd lived in since her arrival in his stratosphere.

It wouldn't mean anything other than a means to soothe their distraught son.

He would be back to being the domineering banker

who'd invaded her habitat with a clutch of law enforcement officers a little over three weeks ago.

Repeating that to herself, she quickly changed Leo's nappy, placed him in his crib, and returned to her room to dress.

She threw on a short floral dress, added low-heeled platform mules and tidied her hair. A glide of lip gloss and she was ready.

She returned to fetch Leo, and was about to pick up his baby bag when Ekow appeared.

He was dressed in hip-hugging jeans and a pristine white polo shirt that made his dark skin glow. Again she diverted her gaze, before she swallowed her tongue, but when he started towards her, to take Leo into his arms, Eva couldn't stop her eyes from returning to him. From watching the entirely too masculine swagger, the unrepressed confidence and the sheer aura of his personality.

'Ready?' he asked, after he'd reached for the bag to take that too.

Eva concluded that all these aberrant feelings were hormonal—probably post-partum. Not because at far too many points after Leo's birth she'd wished that she wasn't undertaking the monumental task of parenting alone. That she wouldn't end up like her mother, utterly resentful of the absence of the men who'd fathered her two children and too bitter to share their details with said children.

'Yes,' she replied.

In silence they went downstairs, via a wide, sweeping staircase, then through the marble-floored hallway and past a pristine, magazine-shoot-ready kitchen and into a garage housing more cars than she could take in in a single glance.

She'd accepted mere days into her arrival that in some aspects her life had changed for ever. It turned out billionaires couldn't just step out on a whim without a multitude of bodyguards in attendance. So she wasn't surprised in the least when four burly men appeared from another door attached to the garage and climbed into sleek black SUVs.

Eva cautioned herself not to be disappointed that this wasn't a cute family of three out for a late-night drive. But she couldn't hide the resurgence of the blasted fizz inside her when Ekow headed towards another, sleeker SUV.

As if he knew he was going on his own personal adventure Leo had quieted a little, his curious eyes rounded as he took in his surroundings.

Ekow opened and held the door for her, then settled Leo in his car seat.

The roads were quiet, a contrast to the incessant traffic which clogged them during the day, and their ride was smooth as they left the city behind. Eva didn't mind the silence. She was too busy trying not to glance at Ekow's capable hands on the steering wheel and the way the muscles in his thighs played beneath the streetlights when he changed gear. Hell, she was too busy using up all her energy in not breathing too deeply, because she felt as if his scent was pulling her closer with each inhalation, inviting her into that sinful space where his essence resided.

'Think it's working?'

She jumped, petrified she'd spoken her feelings aloud. 'What?'

His head turned, his gaze slashing through the dim interior to lock on hers. 'He's quiet. I think the drive's working.'

His son. Of course.

Eva exhaled shakily. They'd just started winding their way up the snake-like roads into the Aburi mountains. She knew that in minutes they'd be treated to spectacular views from the top.

She craned her neck and watched Leo succumb to sleep, his long lashes brushing the tops of his cheeks. 'Yes, it is,' she murmured.

Ekow nodded. 'Good.'

The soporific sensation was threatening to burrow into her when he pulled up to a vantage point at the side of the road. Eva ignored the other two SUVs pulling up on either side of them as Ekow stepped out, left the engine running, and rounded the hood to her side.

She let him help her out and they walked to the edge of the lookout. The air smelled infinitely cleaner and richer, and she took a long, deep breath, her gaze on the twinkling lights that looked magical…near enough to reach out and touch.

Aburi was set into the mountains north-east of Accra, and at this time of night, with a clear starlit sky above, the city was a breathtaking multi-hued carpet of bright lights.

'The view is better from up there,' Ekow said after several minutes.

Eva followed his gaze to where he pointed, but all she

could see was a dark surge of trees and rocks marching up the side of the mountain. 'Where?'

'Come. I'll show you.'

He led her back to the car, taking care not to jostle it and wake Leo.

They travelled even higher. After ten minutes, he stopped in front of high security gates and a wall that soared at least twenty feet high.

He entered a code and electronic gates slid smoothly open, displaying a long, palm-lined, white-stone-paved drive. Strategically placed lights illuminated rolling green grass on either side of the drive, but her gaze was drawn to the large stone-clad building set into the side of the mountain.

The house was smaller than Quayson House but no less grand for it. Every square foot of the outside screamed moneyed elegance which she discovered was repeated on the inside, with a warm cream theme in marble, and furniture and art chosen as if in invitation to enjoy a slower pace, a chance to linger and admire, to lounge and indulge. The sumptuous sofas were made for sprawling, unlike the stately formality of the decor at Quayson House.

With each room they silently walked through, with Ekow effortlessly carrying the sleeping Leo in his car seat, Eva fell in love with the house.

'You own this house?' she murmured.

'Yes.'

She wasn't sure why that both delighted and alarmed her. While she didn't like the sensation of being pulled deeper into Ekow's web of power and influence, she found she didn't particularly mind this silken strand tugging at her. Which was a little disconcerting, considering her determination to stay aloof.

Because she didn't want to risk Leo waking, she remained silent until Ekow set him down in a fully furnished nursery, the sight of which drew two dozen questions, then stepped out and noiselessly shut the door.

'Did you plan to bring us here?'

His lips tightened, then he shrugged. 'Only to show you the view I promised. Shall we?' He waved a hand at the grand staircase leading to the upper floors.

Beautifully carved wooden doors she suspected led to bedrooms were dotted along one long corridor, interspersed with richly woven rugs made traditionally by loom-crafting artisans. At the end of the hall French doors opened out onto the large terrace she'd seen from outside.

Eva's breath caught when she stepped out, her feet compelled to take her to the iron railing.

The view had been breathtaking from a few hundred feet below, but up higher it was beyond magnificent. Perhaps it was made more so by the exclusive location, the feeling that she was being treated to a special, unique view from Ekow's private terrace.

'I'd forgotten how beautiful it is up here in the mountains,' she murmured, unable to tear her gaze from the view.

'When was the last time you visited?'

She tried not to stiffen at the question, despite her words having thrown the door wide open for his speculation. But she knew the tension seizing her stemmed from her reluctance to discuss her mother, not his curiosity. 'You mean before I came here last year, to tell you I was pregnant with our son?'

She sensed him stiffen too, and tiny pangs of guilt and shame pierced her. The ride through the winding hills had been beautiful and serene. She didn't want to wreck it with tension.

When he remained silent, she sighed. 'I last visited when I was twenty-one. I don't remember much of our visits before then. They were always spur-of-the-moment and short when I younger.'

He frowned. 'Why?'

Her back tightened some more. She'd never made a secret of the fact that she and Jonah were each other's only family, as far as she knew. Would he pity her?

She shook her head to dissipate her thoughts. 'I think my mother missed her homeland, but something here made her unhappy. We'd arrive excited but she'd get sad within a couple of days. The trips were always cut short and she never told me why.'

'So you came back when you were old enough to experience it for yourself?'

She nodded. 'I toured Aburi and the rest of the Eastern Region in my first week, and the rest of the country in the four weeks after that.'

'What happened to her?' His voice was a low, even rumble. Filled more with curiosity than interrogation.

Eva tightened her gut against the tug of pain. 'She had a chronic disease—COPD. It worsened over the last six years. She died two years ago.'

Silence reigned for several moments before his hand brushed the back of hers. 'I'm sorry.' The words were gruff…sounded unused. As if he didn't know grief. But hadn't his father died recently?

Eva opened her mouth, perhaps to utter one of the automatic replies to the sympathies people offered in this situation, despite the risk of shattering this somewhat mellow couple of hours they'd enjoyed.

But he beat her to it with another question. 'And your father?'

The hole in her heart where the questions and heartache surrounding her parentage resided squeezed painfully. 'Is not a subject I like to talk about.'

Somehow the hand brushing the back of her hand had found her wrist. Caught in a light hold, it nevertheless snagged her attention, soothing, but making her intensely aware of his warm touch as his fingers caressed her pulse.

'Not to anyone else, maybe. But I'd like to think I have special dispensation as your husband.'

The throb of possessiveness in his voice made her heart skip several beats. 'We're not married yet,' she pointed out, a touch too breathlessly.

He shrugged. 'That's just semantics. I already consider you mine.'

She should've been outraged by that—and she was, somewhere in the murky soup of her emotions, she assured herself. But the subject lying between them like an undetonated bomb wouldn't let her dwell on the currents of electricity zipping beneath her skin.

Hyper-aware of the thumb caressing her inner wrist, she tried to focus on the carpet of lights before her, to lose herself in the view while she chose her words. But in the end it all came tumbling out.

'I don't know my father. Have never met him. For as long as I can remember I've yearned to know. But my mother wouldn't tell me anything. He was in her past, as far as she was concerned, and whatever happened between them was enough for her to cut him out of her life. And mine,' she added, with a layer of bitterness in her words.

'Did you ever try to find him?'

Anguish burned like acid in her heart and seared her throat with tears. She blinked rapidly to dispel it. 'I wouldn't know where to start. I don't have a name. She didn't even give me that.'

That infernal thumb traced her pulse again and her breath shuddered out.

'Maybe she was trying to save you from heartache,' he said, and she caught a note of perplexity in his voice. As if even while he could make the deduction the act was still alien to him. While she fought the knot in her throat, he added, 'Or disappointment.'

This time the note was definitive. Blisteringly so. And it was formed from a tight bundle of bitterness and quiet rage.

It was enough to make her forget her turbulent emotions and turn to him just as he faced her. 'Telling myself that doesn't help,' she said.

His jaw rippled with that same twist of emotion. 'Sometimes nothing helps. The only thing you can do is forget. Or seek escape.'

She gasped. 'You have the world at your beck and call. Why would you need escape?'

'Beds of roses generally have thorns, Evangeline. And some wound deeper than others.'

'What do you mean?'

His strain intensified, and for several seconds he turned away, presenting her with an austere profile. Still, she saw flickers of charged emotion cross his face, so that when he glanced at her again her stomach was clenched in anxiety.

'I mean having two parents present doesn't automatically guarantee a happy bond. You met my father. I probably know the answer, but what were your impressions of him?

Memory tore open in her mind, stinging her anew. 'Not great,' she said tightly.

His lips tightened, his face a bleak mask. 'So at the very least you know he wasn't an…easy man to deal with.'

She licked her lips. 'I thought perhaps he was protecting you from me. Are you saying…?'

'I'm saying that being a Quayson son was…*is* a lot to live up to. And in his eyes I didn't live up to expectations. Neither of his remaining sons did.'

'He played favourites with his sons?'

'Blatantly and without remorse,' he admitted, his tone an arid desert. 'He lived for only one person—his firstborn son.'

The raw confession drew a gasp from her, and her insides grew soft with compassion for him. 'Ekow…'

He shook his head. 'This isn't my way to win your sympathy. It's a way for you to weigh the balance of what you think you've been deprived of with the possibility that you might be better off. If your mother cared for you, perhaps you should be content with having one parent's love instead of none at all.'

She bit her lip, hearing his words, feeling them touch her, but unable to dismiss the coiled pain and loss at not knowing. Would she spend the rest of her life feeling this way?

Torn by her thoughts, by the weird sense of solidarity she felt with him at his painful admission, she turned blindly to him when he stepped close.

'Enough. I don't want to ruin this view and this peace with this subject. Not when I want something else more…'

Her gaze rose. Locked with his. 'What…?' The question was barely a whisper. She stopped breathing as he raised her wrist to his lips and brushed a kiss across it.

'This…'

His free hand slipped around her nape, his thumb trailing down her jaw before tilting her head up to meet his hungry, burning gaze.

Evangeline had more than ample time to pull away, to step back. To nudge a *no* from the jumble of words clogged in her throat. But she did none of those things.

Because she wanted him to kiss her. Wanted to feel his lips on hers. To wipe away the troubling memories she'd dredged up.

She wanted to *feel*.

To feel the way she had that weekend with him in Cape Town. The way she hadn't felt *since*. Because, as she'd feared when she'd stealthily dragged her clothes on at dawn, fearful of waking him and yet almost willing him to rouse and stop her from leaving, Ekow Quayson might have ruined her for any other man.

The thought shook through her anew, convincing her that testing out the theory was prudent. Essential, even. So when he bent lower, his nostrils flaring as he inhaled, she gave a tight, needy moan…

And surged up to meet his decadent lips.

She'd imagined it would be as intoxicating as the first time she'd kissed him. But, no. Ekow was like a fine wine from the renowned Stellenbosch region of western South Africa. He'd matured with time. And like the perfect vintage he swept through her, lowered her inhibitions and invited her in for a third, fourth, *fifth* taste.

Beneath the mesmerising night sky she swayed closer, winding her arms around his neck, revelling in his throaty hum of approval as he drew her even tighter to the steel and flesh masterpiece that was his warm body.

His lips parted hers, deepening the kiss, and every cell in her body seemed to rouse, to strain towards the pleasure only he had been able to deliver.

'You taste even better than I remember,' he rasped, in between nipping her bottom lip and then laving it with his tongue. Repeatedly. Making her shudder. Making her nipples pucker and her breasts ache.

'You remember?' she asked, then immediately regretted it. It made her sound much too needy. Too gauche.

To her surprise and pleasure he murmured again, one hand boldly cupping her breast, moulding, caressing. 'I remember,' he stated thickly. 'You've stayed a vivid memory, Evangeline.'

She ached to explore that statement. But he was toying with her nipple. And she was losing her mind. Which was why she barely registered it when he wrapped one strong arm around her waist and lifted her off her feet, plastering her against the wall beside the French doors seconds later.

One taut thigh slid between hers, and she whimpered when he pressed firmly at the apex of her thighs. His tongue stroked and teased hers, driving her fever higher, making her yearn for him to explore her in other, needier places.

'I definitely haven't forgotten how deliciously responsive you are,' he rasped, his mouth leaving hers to explore the highly sensitive column of her throat.

It was a stronger, more desperate shudder which shook a thread of sanity free. Which dragged open eyes she didn't remember shutting. The ferocious blaze in his eyes nearly undid her.

She was grateful for the breeze that whispered over her skin. And when his head started to descend again she held on to the thread and turned her head. His sinful lips landed on her cheek, began to chart another chaotic path down her neck.

'I... I think that's enough.'

He froze, then one corner of his lips quirked. 'It not nearly enough, sweetheart,' he muttered hoarsely. 'Not for me anyway.'

A moment later she realised his meaning, her breath snagging all over again as his engorged shaft pressed against her belly.

Then he was stepping back, placing cool air between them, and she immediately regretted it. To her eternal relief she didn't reach for him, beg him to disregard her protest and continue. She turned unseeingly for the hallway, not stopping until she stood in the doorway leading to where Ekow had left their sleeping son.

He was still fast asleep and she bit her lip, reluctant
to disturb him. But they needed to leave this peaceful,
magical place that was seeping under her defences, laying fertile soil for dreams she had no right to harbour.

'Here, let me,' Ekow murmured low behind her.

A quick glance showed lingering after-effects of their
passionate tussle—mostly in the bank of fire in his eyes.
But he was back under control. When she gave a jerky
nod he lifted the carrier smoothly, his easy strength
barely rocking it.

Minutes later they were back in the SUV, with the
house growing smaller in the rear-view mirror.

'You're either beating yourself up about wanting
what happened up there or convincing yourself you
didn't want it in the first place. Both are wasted efforts,'
he drawled when they were halfway down the mountain.

'You're a mind-reader now?' she whispered heatedly.

He shrugged. 'I don't need to be. You give yourself
away far too easily, Eva.'

She turned away, literally, from the unwanted truth,
staring out of the window as the lights of the city—and
her wedding—grew closer.

The smooth ride must have lulled her into a doze.
The next thing she knew she was being lowered into
her own bed. She roused herself with a start, staring
into Ekow's dark brown eyes. 'Leo…?'

He pressed her down. 'Is fine. He's already in his
crib. Transferring him was a delicate operation, but I
managed it. Just about.'

What did it say about her that she'd been completely
oblivious to all of it?

Ekow sighed as he straightened, his gaze hardening

at whatever he read in her face. 'I'm sensing a theme here. I guess I'll need to wean you off this "me against the world" mentality you have.'

'It's not a mentality if it's true.'

For endless moments he stared at her. The passionate, attentive man she'd tangled with a short hour ago was gone. The eyes raking her were still heated, but the fire was nowhere near as ferocious. Or warming.

And it felt decidedly less so when he took another step back.

'I'm going to be busy the next few days. I'll see you at the altar.'

'What if I don't make it there?' she threw defiantly at him, attempting to claw back the ground she hadn't even been aware she'd lost to him.

He didn't so much as blink in response. 'You will,' he stated with enviable assurance. 'Unfortunately for you, angel, you won't get rid of me that easily. Sleep well.'

His voice held enough sardonicism to tell her that neither of them would sleep well after the state they'd left things in. After their earth-shaking kiss.

But she managed to stop her runaway tongue from inciting further emotional wreckage. It'd done quite enough for one night.

So she watched him leave, his magnetising presence taking every essence of her being with him as he shut the door calmly behind him.

To alleviate the sudden loss, Eva dragged a pillow close, hugged it as she tried to calm her roiling senses. But one fundamental reality kept echoing in her head.

They might have set out settle their distraught son, but what she'd just proved to herself was that when it came to her emotions around the man who had fathered her child, things were far from settled.

Hell, they were even more volatile than she'd thought.

CHAPTER EIGHT

EVA HADN'T IMAGINED her wedding day.

So of course she hadn't entertained the idea of being nervous to the point of nausea. Or of accommodating butterflies the size of small birds in her belly from the moment the veil was placed on her head and the exquisite bouquet, the stem of which was wrapped in ribbons of colourful Kente cloth, was placed in her hand.

All around her a contingent of Quayson females were dressed to the nines. The traditional Ghanaian wear of the rich and boldly coloured *kaba* and *slit*, with elaborate matching headdresses, was interspersed with westernised wedding attire, while stunning jewellery and accessories provided bursts of colour. It was almost too overwhelming to take in.

She wallowed in a momentary well of sadness that neither her mother nor Jonah was here before she shook it off. While not entirely sure what her mother would have made of this, Eva wanted to believe she would've given her blessing.

Breathing through the swell of anxiety, she followed the procession of cutely dressed flower girls and page boys, whose attire followed the theme of blending traditional attire with tiny tulle gowns and tuxedos, to the terrace of Ekow's home, beyond which the sprawling, immaculately landscaped garden now seating several hundred guests awaited her arrival.

Clamping her hand around the bouquet to stop the shaking, she deliberately kept her gaze low to avoid searching out her soon-to-be husband.

True to his word, he'd absented himself from the mansion in the last few days. If she hadn't known better, Evangeline would've thought he was avoiding her. But it was more as if after their ride into the mountains, seeing the magical view from his house and *that kiss*, he'd been content to retreat with her bluff called, knowing she wouldn't...*couldn't* do anything but honour their agreement.

It had worked, hadn't it?

Hadn't she spent countless hours weighing the wisdom of reneging on her agreement against every emotional advantage she could give Leo by going through with this wedding?

And what about your own advantage?

Eva shook her head, unwilling to admit that their kiss replayed far too frequently in her mind, and that the other challenge Ekow had thrown her—about how she would want more from their marriage, specifically things of the carnal kind—had interrupted her thoughts way too much for her liking.

But... She pursed her lips. She'd been completely fine without sex before she met him. She'd be completely fine for however long this marriage lasted.

Liar.

Enough.

Time to get this show on the road.

She'd chosen to walk down the aisle on her own, a decision and a last grasp at independence no amount of disapproving looks from Ekow's mother or the clicking tongues of his various aunts and cousins could sway her from.

Still, stepping out into the blinding sunlight and being confronted with a multitude of curious eyes, Eva wished for a moment she'd insisted Jonah be here at her side. Or accepted Atu's offer to escort her.

Beneath the short veil, she lifted her chin. She could do this. She'd given birth alone, despite being terrified of what the future would bring for her and her son.

The strains of music played by a renowned Ghanaian cellist said to have played at the last English royal wedding signalled the start of the wedding, and she made her practised progress in time with the hiplife tune.

Eva was thankful for the shield of her veil as her gaze avoided the altar and instead searched through the crowd until she found Leo.

He was dressed in the cutest tuxedo, the dark grey colour matching his father's. She'd expected him to be fussing but, surprising her again, he remained calm, taking in everything with wide-eyed interest. Currently perched on his grandmother's lap, he occasionally glanced at the father he was now bonding with at a rate of knots. Eva would have been jealous if she hadn't been so pleased for her son.

In fact, walking down the aisle, surrounded by people she didn't know but who were kin to her son, she finally accepted that she'd done the right thing. He would never feel lonely or overwhelmed at making the choices she'd had to make when her mother's health had started to fail. He would always have support.

A different kind of lump wedged in her throat—the mingled pride and dismay that came from putting another's needs above one's own—and repeatedly caught her in the chest.

Finally she let her gaze be compelled to the figure at the altar. The one she'd been avoiding because she knew she wasn't anywhere near prepared. Perhaps never would be.

Despite clenching her gut against it, the punch still arrived, and his magnificent form and impressive presence instantly blocked out everything else.

Because Ekow in a morning suit, his designer stubble expertly trimmed and his entire focus on her, was more than enough to interrupt the steady, practised glide of her feet.

His gaze was blatantly possessive. Feverishly fixed on her in a way that roused every dormant sexual cell into rude life.

I already consider you mine.

Telling herself he didn't own her was pitifully inadequate. Because his gaze announced differently. He might have accepted her 'no sex' clause as part of this convenient marriage, but he didn't intend to remain detached. At least not in public.

Those words throbbed in time to her heartbeat. In time to the intensity in his eyes. And no amount of telling herself it was all for show could stop the trembling that seized her then and continued through their vows, through the glide of his ring onto her finger, and especially through the feeling, as he repeated his promise to her, that she was taking a road from which there would be no return.

Eva took solace in counting the hours. In knowing that within twenty-four hours things would go back to being relatively normal.

Ekow would return to the challenging demands of running Quayson Bank and she would be left to bring up her son in peace. Or as peacefully as her disapproving mother-in-law would allow.

She was still reassuring herself about that when, her hand tucked into her new husband's, they arrived at the grand salon in Quayson House, where the reception was being held.

The new gold band weighed heavy on her finger. She knew the nugget it had been formed from had been mined from his family's gold mine a decade ago and set aside for this occasion because her mother-in-law had informed her of it, with a lofty sniff that had suggested Evangeline should fall to her knees and be overawed.

She'd settled on a serene smile instead.

Several long banquet tables groaning under the weight of exquisite food were positioned around the room. Mouthwatering jollof rice, rice and beans, *kpekple* with king crab. All beautifully complemented with various rich sauces and meats roasting on a dozen spits, and exclusively labelled spirits flowing alongside the locally brewed *asana* and palm wine.

Evangeline had a vague notion that had this been a common social gathering she would've enjoyed herself. But it wasn't. She was a stranger here—and not a particularly wanted one.

As she discovered when she excused herself an hour

into the reception to visit the powder room and met the cool eyes of the woman there, poised in front of the mirror.

Tall, statuesque, she wore a stunning purple outfit that made her flawless skin glow. She approached Eva on high heels, the gentle flare of her hips and her endless legs announcing her supermodel status. From a sleek purse she pulled a tube of lipstick, but made no move to refresh her make-up. Instead, she speared Evangeline with a look that was a cross between pity and envy.

'Well played, sis.'

'Excuse me?'

The woman launched a tight smile through the mirror. 'You've achieved what many women would give a limb for. You've landed the last eligible Quayson. Be careful, though, that you're not playing out of your league. The Quayson men are notoriously hard to please.'

Eva opened her mouth to tell her she hadn't set out to *land* anyone. That claiming his son and heir was her new husband's main goal, and she'd merely been swept along in his unstoppable endeavour. But Ekow's warning that this marriage was to appear real echoed in her head and stilled her tongue. So she summoned another serene smile, and rose above it.

'Thanks for the warning. I hope you enjoy the rest of my wedding.'

She sailed out with her head held high, thankful that her simple, elegant dress made walking much easier than one of the fuller, more elaborate gowns Ekow's mother had been pushing on her would have.

Ekow's gaze zeroed in on her the moment she stepped back into the room, and it was like a flash of lightning through her system, making her shakier still by the time she arrived at the chair he'd pulled out for her.

'You should eat something,' he murmured in her ear as she took her seat.

The very thought of it made her stomach roil. 'I'm not very hungry,' she said, reaching for her glass of mineral water.

'I thought wedding nerves were supposed to occur *before* the ceremony, not after?'

She shrugged. 'Maybe I'm an exception to all the rules.'

Expecting a mocking response, she was stunned when his face grew circumspect. 'Perhaps you are,' he concurred with a rasp that sent a frisson of something dancing over her. 'You walking down the aisle on your own certainly flouted a rule. But I find that not knowing what to expect from you next is…interesting.'

She bit her tongue against asking if that was a good or a bad thing. She didn't want to know. But the heated gleam in his eyes which remained whether they were talking about the weather or debating the wisdom of a fiery kiss called her a liar.

She wanted him to be interested.

Eva swallowed against the foolish notion as he continued to watch her, continued to assess her like a juicy deal he was seriously contemplating landing.

The atmosphere grew thick, the steady rise and fall of his chest mocking the rapid agitation of hers.

Beyond her peripheral vision his older brother and best man stood and made a speech Eva barely heard, drawing applause she absently smiled at as Ekow's gaze clung to hers, asking questions she wasn't ready to answer.

Then the first dance was announced.

The mild panic in her midriff grew as he rose to his feet and held out a large, forthright hand to her.

They'd touched exactly three times since she'd met him at the altar. When he'd placed the ring on her finger, when he had been invited to kiss the bride and he'd taken hold of her, drawing her to him and placing a firm but short kiss on her lips that had nevertheless set her whole body tingling. And when they'd walked down the aisle after exchanging their vows.

The rest of the time he'd been courteous but physically distant.

And now she was supposed to sail into his arms, pretend she was ecstatic…

She took his hand, unable to disguise its tremble, an action he took note of, if the slight tightening of his own fingers was a sign.

'If you get any stiffer you'll break into little pieces, dear wife,' he murmured, close enough for her to feel his breath on the shell of her ear. Close enough to make her shiver when his lip brushed the top of her ear.

'It's hard to relax when a thousand eyes are watching you.'

'They stare because you look exquisite,' he stated, with a lofty arrogance which should've set her teeth on edge but only made something vital inside her melt, then catch fire, as if it wanted to compete with the smouldering look in his eyes. 'They stare because they envy you,' he added, his hands gently guiding her across the grand salon floor to the strains of another Hip Life masterpiece from the cellist. 'And if it bothers you, then know that you only need to be concerned with *my* eyes.'

But your eyes are the worst... They make me...yearn.

She kept the response inside, of course. Because none of that was part of their deal. 'Thanks for the compliment. But it won't surprise you to know I can't wait for all this to be over.'

His hands tightened momentarily around her waist, then eased just as quickly. But the sharpness in his eyes intensified. He watched her for several seconds before he gave a short nod, with a look of annoyingly supreme understanding in his eyes. 'You're understandably overwhelmed. It will pass soon enough, once we're on our way.'

She jerked slightly in his arms. 'On our way where?'

Although his face stayed carefully neutral she saw a glint of displeasure in his eyes. 'I had one of my assistants email you our itinerary. Should I be concerned that you didn't look at it?'

'I've been too busy to check my personal emails. And excuse me if I've not brushed up on the etiquette of being married to billionaires who communicate with their wives through assistants and emails. I prefer face-to-face communication myself.'

For some reason that made his lips twitch. 'Are we having our first marital fight, Evangeline? When we haven't even finished our first dance yet?'

His reference to their union didn't stem the rising tide of panic. Nor did the dangerous quirking of his lips in amusement.

'It's not much of a fight when one party seems infinitely amused, is it?' she asked.

'Perhaps amusement is one option.'

Something about the timbre of his tone unfurled another flare of heat inside her. 'And another is what, exactly?'

He stepped back, took her hand and swung her around, before expertly catching her in his arms again. 'Scandalise you by kissing that sassy mouth until neither of us can see straight,' he said, almost conversationally.

She tightened her defences against what his suave moves and his words did to her. 'You have my thanks for not choosing the less sensible option, then.'

His smile this time looked strained up close. 'Being sensible is the last thing on my mind when I think about kissing you, wife.'

Before she could respond, the music slowed to a melodic end. She forced a smile at the rapturous applause and let him lead her off the dance floor.

When he was promptly claimed by a small crowd of relatives and friends Eva almost breathed sigh of relief, and then the wedding co-ordinator discreetly approached, asking whether she would like anything special packed, she was reminded her that she hadn't discovered where they were going.

She was tempted to ask the wedding co-ordinator, but what would it say about her if she confessed she had no clue what her own husband had planned?

Responding that, no, she didn't want anything special, she made her way back to the table, where a flagging Leo was doing his best to stay awake. The middle-aged nanny, who'd started watching him whenever Eva had been required for wedding preparations, looked up and smiled.

'He's just had his bottle. I was about to go and get him ready for your trip, Mrs Quayson.'

Eva started, something desperately needy catching in her midriff at the new form of address. 'Please, call me Eva.'

The woman smiled again and nodded, before her gaze swung over her shoulder. Eva didn't need to look to know Ekow was close. Her very skin fired up at his proximity. Eva placed a lingering kiss on her son's head, then stepped back and watched, feeling something moving deep in her chest, as Ekow drew close and did the same.

Once they were alone, Ekow turned to her. 'Almost time to say our goodbyes.'

She'd been feverishly counting the hours and minutes before. Now, hearing the throb of…*something* in his voice, she wished she could stop time.

'You didn't tell me where we're going.'

He stepped close, caught up her hand and, uncaring of the avid eyes fixed on them, brushed his lips over her knuckles. 'We're going on our honeymoon, Evangeline. Where else?'

Paris and Cape Verde were the eventual destinations for her honeymoon, Eva found out two hours later when, after finding herself alone for a scant five minutes when the stylist left her to change, she frantically searched her emails.

But first they were travelling by helicopter to a private resort in Axim, where they'd spend the night, before returning to Accra and heading for Paris.

The forty-five-minute flight saw them land on the edge of a breathtaking beach just as the sun was setting on golden thatch-roofed chalets and winding pathways.

'What is this place? It's stunning,' she gushed as Ekow helped her into a sleek little tender, handed Leo over, and aided the nanny.

He smiled, her response obviously pleasing him. 'It's a set of ten eco-lodges. Three, including the one we're using, are set on their own islands.'

Their island was no bigger than a tennis court, but the chalet looked directly onto a serene beach with swaying palm trees and golden sand. 'How did I not know about this place? I scoured information on hundreds of places to stay when I visited the last time,' she said from the balcony, after she'd helped the nanny put Leo to bed.

Ekow came towards her, handing her a glass of fruit punch. Like her, he'd changed into less formal clothes, and his open-necked shirt was being caressed by the setting sun, giving her mouthwatering glimpses of his strong throat.

'It's only a year old. I only knew about it because Atu's was dying to get his hands on it.'

She frowned. 'And he didn't succeed? That's unlike him…' She'd only known her brother-in-law a short time, but the Quayson fortitude was as alive and present in him as it was in his younger brother.

Ekow strolled away and returned with a platter of seafood, pointedly holding it out to her. Perhaps it was the ocean air, or her magnificent surroundings, but her appetite suddenly roared back. She took a bite of grilled prawn and melon and moaned under her breath.

Ekow's smile widened, his eyes heating up. 'He tried. I beat him to the punch.'

Her eyes widened. 'You own this place?'

'Not any more.' Reaching into his back pocket, he drew out a thick folded piece of paper. 'It's yours now. My wedding present to you.'

She nearly dropped her glass. 'I… What? I can't—'

His fingers brushed her lips, freezing her words. 'You can. You will. I'm not taking it back.'

'But… I didn't get you anything.'

A fierce light gleamed in his eyes. 'You've given me Leo. But if you're offering more…'

The husky rasp in his voice had her stepping back, afraid of the spark of her own yearning. 'No. I said… We agreed…'

His lips twisted. 'And I gave us a month before we succumbed. Well, here we are. Let's see how we do, hmm?'

That clear intent lingered for the rest of the evening as they ate, drank, and pointedly steered away from lustful subjects; even as they changed into their night-clothes and headed for the one, albeit large and sump-tuous, bed in the chalet.

As she and her new husband slid into bed, then lay staring at the ceiling on this their wedding night, thick ropes of sensuality slowly coiled around them and, almost inevitably, reminding her of their weekend in Cape Town. Reminding her that Ekow was the only man she'd slept with.

The only man, she suspected alarmingly, she'd ever want to sleep with.

* * *

Because everything had gone like clockwork so far, Eva didn't doubt their transition from Axim back to Quayson House before they headed to the airport would happen at the allotted time.

Dressed in a sleeveless cream silk jumpsuit with a waist-length African print cape of a similar colour-scheme tossed over it, she fixed her hair and caught up her bag.

Several suitcases were packed, ready to be stowed in the SUVs heading for the airport. The nanny approached her in the hallway with Leo in her arms and Ekow's mother next to them.

Naana Quayson's gaze was cool, approaching chilling. Eva still had no idea why the older woman disliked her, save the glaring fact that she wasn't the woman Mrs Quayson had chosen, and had apparently spent considerable time and effort matchmaking for her remaining single son.

Short of actually saying what she'd considered telling the beautiful stranger in the powder room yesterday, all she could do was smile. 'Everything went perfectly yesterday. Thank you.'

Ekow's mother looked momentarily stunned, as if she hadn't expected the courtesy. But that smallest hint of warmth soon disappeared, leaving the coolness Eva had come to expect.

'My son deserves the best, so that's exactly what I delivered. I don't need thanks from *you* for that.'

As usual, the warm, joyous weight of Leo lifted Eva's spirits, and she pressed a kiss to his cheek before she looked at her mother-in-law. 'Well, we're a family now, so what you do for him, you do for me.'

The moment the words spilled from her mouth she knew she'd taken the wrong tack. But of course she couldn't take them back.

Naana Quayson's face tightened further, disdain crossing her face before, glancing at the silent nanny, she replaced it with neutrality. 'Enjoy your honeymoon,' she said stiffly.

The unspoken *while it lasts* lingered in the air, following Eva downstairs and into the first of the fleet of SUVs waiting to whisk them to the airport.

For the first ten minutes Eva stared at the passing scenery, letting father and son entertain each other.

'Something troubling you? Or is the silent treatment for crimes I'm unaware of?' asked Ekow.

Her intention of staying silent lasted only a nanosecond. 'I'm not sure who hates me more—your mother, or all the women out there who'd hoped to become the last Mrs Quayson.'

He stiffened, turning to face her. 'Did she say something to you?' he bit out.

Eva shrugged. 'Words weren't necessary.'

His jaw gritted for a moment before he relaxed. 'Letting go isn't easy for her, I suspect. No doubt you'll feel the same about our son?'

'Or maybe it isn't that at all,' she blurted. 'She clearly thinks you've made a mistake. That seems to be the general consensus, doesn't it?' Eva hadn't realised how much that chafed until the words fell between them.

'The "general consensus" is irrelevant. And none

of those women are the mother of my child,' he responded tightly.

Just like that a chill swept over her, icing over every ember she'd been foolish enough to leave flaming 'Of course. How can I forget my unique position?'

'If you want me to say otherwise then you're going to be disappointed.' He exhaled noisily, then his gaze probed hers deeper in the dim interior. 'Do you want more, Evangeline? Is that what this is about? Because if it is, you only have to—'

'It isn't.'

Her voice had emerged firmly enough to fool even her. Was that a flash of disappointment in his eyes? She couldn't tell because his lashes swept down, then away, his focus once more on Leo.

'Then what are we arguing about?'

The chafing turned into a deep burn, eating away at the edges of her heart. 'Nothing at all.'

Nothing at all.

Ekow was more disturbed by those three words than he cared to admit.

For reasons he was at a loss to name, Evangeline was disrupting his previously exemplary thought processes.

Take those few moments during his wedding, for example, when he'd entertained the same idea he'd had that first night last month, after seeing her again.

He'd forgotten himself. Forgotten the infernal agreement he'd made with his new wife not to claim her in the most intimate way.

Seeing her walk down the aisle towards him in the classy yet deeply sensual dress he'd chosen and she'd picked for herself, he'd been thrown back to their first meeting. And to their evening in Aburi, when he'd kissed her. When he'd felt a strange peace with her he'd never felt with another.

More than her ethereal beauty and the memory of the sex and the passion, it had been seeing her turn up at all. Yes, he'd called her bluff after that trip. How could he not have? He'd stared into the face of rejection so many times with his father, he'd learned the deep art of the poker face. He'd learned to face up to the possibility of loss and rejection before it came, rather than wait to be gutted by it when he least expected it.

Eva rose to a challenge, he'd learned. So he'd dared her to turn up at the altar.

Watching her stride down alone and yet fiercely proud, he'd once again toyed with the idea of...*more*.

Now he knew that idea wasn't a viable one.

She didn't seem to want what every other woman before her had craved—power, money, prestige, and not necessarily in that order. All she truly cared about was her brother and their son.

He stared at his beautiful boy, the child he now believed she'd intended to tell him about all along, and wondered if there was a way to alter things between them.

As they pulled up to the Quayson private jet he glanced at the woman who now bore his name. Considered the possibility that she really wasn't like most women. That she'd set out simply to do the right thing and wanted nothing from him.

Nothing at all...

Just like his father?

He gritted his jaw, displeased by his thoughts circling back to the one person he didn't want to think about today.

Ekow ignored the taunting inner voice and stepped out, unbuckling his son before taking control of his carrier.

When Eva stepped out, her eyes widening on his jet, he felt a punch of satisfaction. It was a mildly fatuous thought, but if, like with her wedding gift, he could dazzle her a little more, perhaps she might see her way to…

What?

Forgetting every accusation he'd thrown at her in Cape Town?

And then what?

Dazzle her some more? Coax her into his bed? Sex for the sake of it?

When he would've given a resounding *yes* somewhere in the not so distant past, now Ekow's insides twisted at the idea, a hollow feeling chasing fast on its heels.

That thought of *more* he'd entertained punched harder, insisting on recognition he couldn't give it.

He glanced down at Eva as he led her and their son towards his plane.

Or could he?

CHAPTER NINE

Eva landed in Paris with a different man.

Where there'd been distance before, there was none now. Ekow even took her hand as they stepped off the plane at Paris Charles de Gaulle Airport, and didn't release it as they got into another SUV that took them to the heart of the city.

She wanted to ask him what he was playing at, but the words stuck in her throat. The idea that she didn't want to know because she *liked* it was all too real as they were transferred from the vehicle to a penthouse suite.

The grand hotel on Avenue George V, part of the Quayson Hotel Group, oozed jaw-dropping elegance and luxury. From the centuries-old chandeliers to the sparkling marble floors and the courteous butlers and smiling staff, Evangeline was quietly awed by it all.

When Ekow caressed her wrist her objections stuck in her throat as they were shown to a multi-level three-bedroom penthouse, with a master suite some distance from the other two, she started to believe she was in trouble. The views alone were mesmerising—the Eiffel Tower so close she could almost reach out and touch it.

With Leo quickly settled in his crib, and the nanny tucked away in her own room, she found herself alone in the living room, her gaze on the stunning view. But she knew the moment Ekow walked into the room.

Her gaze, utterly compelled, swung to follow his stride across the plush pale gold carpet.

'Are you tired?' he asked.

She shook her head. 'Sleeping on the plane was probably not a good idea. I'm wide awake now.'

He shrugged. 'I've arranged for dinner here in the suite. Or we could go out if you prefer?'

She glanced out of the window, the sight too magnificent and inviting to be denied. 'I'd like to go out, if you don't mind?'

He shook his head. 'Of course not. That, too, is already arranged.'

She glanced down at the clothes she'd worn to travel. 'I'll go and change.'

Walking into the suite she believed was to be hers, she stopped at the sight of the bare dressing room. Turning, she approached the open doorway of the master suite.

Ekow, with the same intent of changing, had removed his shirt and was in the process of toeing off his shoes when she entered the room. The sight of his naked torso froze her in place, her mouth drying as she stared at his chest, at the ripple of his abs as he reached for his belt.

One eyebrow quirked when he saw her.

'I… I think my suitcases have been put here by mistake.'

A tic throbbed in his jaw. 'It wasn't a mistake. I didn't correct the assumption made by the staff that we're sharing a suite since we're newly married. The question is, do you want to fight about it now or later, after dinner?' he asked sardonically.

She raised her chin but couldn't dismiss the waves of heat rolling through her at the sight of his hard-packed body. 'My things will need to be moved, but I don't want to fight. Not right now, anyway.'

'Good. Neither do I. Your clothes are in there.'

Eva bit her lip, realising she wasn't blasé enough to stride across the room to the dressing room when there was a half-naked man, albeit her own husband, within touching distance.

But other than changing her mind and going out to dinner in the jumpsuit she'd travelled in, she had no choice but to head to the dressing room, striding dangerously close to his mind-bending perfection. While he watched her all the way.

The smooth efficiency of the staff was evident in the already unpacked and tidily put away clothes.

Plucking a neat little cerise number off its hangar, she quickly gathered the accessories she needed. And then stopped. The idea of scurrying away to dress out of sight when they already had an established agreement irritated her.

The faint sounds of the shower made up her mind for her.

Quickly undressing, she pulled on the thigh-skimming wraparound dress, trying not to imagine Ekow next door, water cascading down his chiselled body.

She slid her feet into silver diamante strapless heels and added the accessories she'd selected. While she hadn't asked for it, she was grateful for the new wardrobe included with her wedding apparel, although the labels on the dresses and accessories made her jaw drop.

Eva didn't think there'd ever come a time when she'd got used to the staggering wealth attached to the man she'd married. Perhaps it was a good thing, since this marriage came with a use-by date anyway.

She ignored the way her stomach dipped, and concentrated on refreshing her make-up before Ekow emerged from the bathroom. She'd just tucked her phone and lipstick into her silver clutch bag when he entered the dressing room.

The towel wrapped around his waist rode low enough to make her tongue swell in her mouth, the sudden rush of craving stinging her core.

He either didn't notice her reaction, or he didn't care that he was half naked in her presence as he strode across the room to his side of the dressing area.

Realising she was still gaping at him after several seconds, Eva whirled around and headed for the door.

'Evangeline...'

The husky utterance of her full name stopped her in her tracks.

She glanced over her shoulder, almost too terrified to look at his body again. 'Yes?'

'You look breathtaking,' he said thickly, his gaze conducting a searing head-to-toe scrutiny before meeting her eyes.

Eva swallowed. The thick lust in the air threatened to suffocate her but she was sure she would die happy. All the more reason to get out of there—fast.

'I... Thank you.'

He gave an arrogant half-smile and continued to look

deep into her eyes for another few moments before he turned away and started to drop his towel.

She fled.

By the time he joined her in the living room fifteen minutes later, she'd managed to get herself under some semblance of control.

'I've just checked on Leo. He's sleeping soundly. He shouldn't wake up before morning.'

Eva knew she was rambling, attempting to cover up the electricity zinging between them, but she couldn't help herself. She had to dissipate it somehow before it swallowed her whole.

Her attempt to do was reduced to ash when he threaded his fingers through hers. Her resistance died even before she'd taken her next breath. Whatever was happening here was greater than her willpower could sustain.

And, really, what was the harm in letting him hold her hand? They were in the most romantic city in the world, and it *was* technically their honeymoon.

Ignoring the voice cautioning her about treading on dangerous ground, Eva followed him into the lift.

They walked a few streets to the restaurant he'd chosen, with Eva doing her best to ignore the bodyguards trailing behind them. Perhaps someday she would accept the fact that her husband didn't go anywhere without serious security, but she suspected it would be a long while yet.

Her husband.

He was behaving in every sense like a real husband would, smiling at her across the dining table set in an intimate corner of a restaurant discreetly announcing its double Michelin star status with a plaque beside the door.

He ordered premium exquisite canapés which he shared with her. She chose a lobster bisque which he sampled shamelessly, his smouldering eyes faintly amused when she expressed outrage.

Eva knew she was sinking deeper into the quagmire, risking an emotional attachment she couldn't afford and heading towards the same mistake she'd made last time.

But…no…

That weekend had brought her Leo, the one thing in the universe she loved above everything else.

'You're pensive. Something wrong with the food? Or the company?' he asked, his amusement edged with something more serious now. More circumspect.

'I'm remembering that sitting down to eat with you comes with a price,' she divulged, before she could stop herself.

His face hardened a touch. 'A price that has never been forced on you.'

She shook her head. 'No.'

Because it was the truth. Whatever she'd done up to this point had been done with her eyes wide open. It was unfair to blame him for any of it. Sure, some of the choices had been less favourable than others, but she'd always had a choice.

Just as she had a choice in whatever was happening now…?

When her attempt to shrug away the question didn't make it go, Eva decided to embrace it. She accepted it when they were finished eating and Ekow led her down a few more streets, then descended steps leading to a promenade that wound alongside the Seine.

Her heart tumbled when she saw his hardened expression hadn't disappeared. But she walked with him in silence, taking in the magnificent city at night and attempting to calm her own agitation.

'You were right,' he stated heavily.

Her heart tumbled a little further, straining towards her toes. 'About what?'

'My father. Your visit. All of it.'

Eva felt something sharp catch in her throat. She swallowed three times before she could speak. 'You looked into it?' She wasn't sure whether she was disappointed or elated at the vindication. Because his revelation meant he hadn't believed her in the first place.

He nodded, having no idea he was deepening whatever this peculiar feeling was rushing through her. 'I couldn't not.'

Eva darted another glance at him. The timbre of his voice was urging her to see things from his perspective. 'You didn't do it because you didn't believe me, did you? You did it for your own reasons?' she surmised.

He didn't answer for an age, his bleak profile turned away, his dark eyes watching a fully lit riverboat slide slowly through the waves, throwing sparkling lights on the murky water. 'Yes,' he eventually admitted.

'Why?'

The gaze that met hers was full of expressions too dark to decipher. 'Because I needed further proof of what I've always known. That I was a mere pawn in whatever game he was playing.'

She gasped. 'Surely that's not true?'

'Why? Because a parent would never do that?'

She opened her mouth to say yes, then closed it. She had no comparison except with her own mother, and even in her most desolate moments her mother had stayed loving to her and Jonah. She'd given them all the support she could, and besides her withholding her father's identity from her it had been enough.

Was Ekow right? *Had* she had it better than some—perhaps even him, despite his wealth, power and prestige—and not appreciated it?

He gave a grim smile, perhaps intuiting her thoughts, and then his gaze once more veered off into the distance, as if meeting hers was too much. As if he was putting distance between them again.

He shrugged. 'Maybe that's not entirely right. My eldest brother wasn't a pawn. He was the rook my father pinned all his hopes on.'

Her heart twisted. 'Your brother…the one who died?'

Ekow gave her another grim nod. 'Yes, he died. Atu had no interest in replacing him. And I…'

'You wanted to be more than a pawn. You wanted to be useful. You wanted the regard every child deserves from its parents.'

He turned sharply to her, his eyes narrowing on her face. 'I just wanted not to be invisible. Nothing more, nothing less. Not to feel as if I didn't matter. Sometimes I'd wonder why he'd wanted more than one child, when it was clear he couldn't find it in himself to…' He paused, his jaw clenching.

'Did you talk to him about it? I know pushing for answers doesn't always work…' she gave a dry laugh, recalling own vain efforts '…but maybe…' She trailed off when he shook his head.

'We didn't have that sort of relationship. Whatever paternal emotions he had were reserved for his golden boy. For the longest time I wondered if that was how it was meant to be. But then I discovered that my cousins and friends had siblings who were all treated equally, so I thought…' Again he stopped.

'You thought it was your fault?' she murmured.

His eyes probed hers. After several tense seconds he sighed. 'How could I not?'

She nodded. 'I thought the same too, when my mother refused to tell me about my father. I thought perhaps I'd done something to make him not want to know me.'

He reached for her hand, a resolute look in his eyes. 'This is why we won't give Leo a moment's doubt about how much he's wanted—yes?'

Her throat clogged and she grappled with an urge to throw her arms around him, to show him every gratifying emotion she felt at his loving their son as much as she did.

'Yes,' she answered hoarsely.

His free hand rose to her face, his knuckles tracing her cheek. She watched as the dull embers in his eyes slowly roused to life. 'My father had no right to deny me my child. No right to treat you the way he did. For that, I'm sorry.'

A tight knot—one that'd been clenched for endlessly long months—eased. When she could speak past the lump in her throat, she asked, 'Why did he do it?'

The question had plagued her for weeks, until she'd

been forced to put it out of my mind for the sake of her sanity and caring for the baby she'd carried.

'Probably because he was distrusting and sceptical, and believed money was the answer to everything,' Ekow said. 'I'm surprised he didn't try to buy you off. He'd done so many times before, with others.'

She winced, her heart plummeting. She opened her mouth to tell him he had, that she'd kept the cheque as a reminder. But looking into his eyes, seeing the anguish his father had caused, Eva couldn't find it in her heart to pile on more heartache. Perhaps someday soon she'd tell him, when things weren't so raw.

Ignoring the warning echoing at the back of her mind, she focused as he continued.

'He was a powerful and influential man with rigid views. He wanted to rule over every inch of our lives. A possible grandchild he didn't know about was out of his control. He acted the only way he knew how, by making sure the problem went away.'

She didn't understand Ekow's father's motives for what he'd done but, God help her, she couldn't help the aching of her heart for the painful childhood Ekow had experienced.

'What about your mother? Didn't she do anything?'

'She was equally under his thumb.' He shrugged. 'Or perhaps she found her own peace in being a compliant wife. I've never stopped to analyse it.'

Eva frowned, certain there was more to it. 'But your relationship with her…?'

'Is better than it used to be. But it'll never be what I want it to be. I know that now.'

'What does that mean?'

He shook his head. 'It means I'm more interested in the family I have now. The family you and I are in the process of creating.'

Her heart lurched. 'But we aren't—'

'But we could be,' he pressed, cupping her shoulders to draw her close enough so she could see the determination in his face. 'You want me. I know you're not contrary enough to deny it.'

She raised an eyebrow, despite her heart banging against her ribs hard enough to drown out the sounds of the city. 'Is that a bluff or a double bluff?'

The smile she'd expected didn't materialise, and his eyes continued to burn into hers. 'Eva…' Again, there were questions and promises in those eyes, warnings and passion. 'Don't condemn us both to celibacy when it doesn't have to be that way.'

Both. Her heart leapt, because at the back of her mind she had always wondered if his words to her that day in Cape Town had been mere talk. But she needed to be sure.

'You mean you don't intend to…?' She licked her lips, stifling a moan when his gaze dropped to linger on her tingling flesh.

'No, I don't. There is no honour in infidelity.'

This moment. This cataclysmic moment when a handful of words could shift her foundations permanently. Underpinning them with fragile hope and whispers of dreams that might not come true but dreams she couldn't pull herself away from.

'Tell me you want this too,' he insisted fervently.

Her lips parted before she could stop herself, but

thankfully the words failed to emerge. Because she needed a moment. Several moments.

To see past the magic of the city and the overwhelming presence of Ekow to the truth in her heart.

To accept that she wanted this. That she'd always wanted this.

Neither her son nor her brother featured in this decision. It was hers alone. Hers to claim. Hers to keep.

For as long as it lasted?

She pushed away that final question. Looked up into the eyes of her husband of one day and said, 'Yes.'

For an age, he simply stared at her. Then he nodded. 'Yes.'

She was thankful he didn't ask for reaffirmation. Not because she wouldn't have given it, but because she was impatient to get to the heart of her needs.

He drew one strong arm around her, binding her waist with his other arm, plastering her against his lithe body. She sighed, her body a willing vessel, all too eager to strain up onto her tiptoes, eager for the kiss he gifted her a moment later.

The kiss, right there on the banks of the Seine, was the stuff of magic. The way his lips claimed hers, his tongue stroking deep inside her mouth, to fulfil every passionate fantasy she'd ever had, was enough to rob her of thought.

Eva didn't care that they were in public and were probably a spectacle for indulgent smiles or scandalised whispers. Wrapping her arms around his waist, she pulled him closer, holding on for dear life as he swept her away, mind and soul.

She swayed when he pulled back, his eyes burning

flames of passion as he captured her hand with his. 'We're returning to the hotel. Now,' he stated gruffly.

She nodded eagerly. Let him pull her along as they rushed back to the penthouse.

Eva gave a laugh of delight when he swung her into his arms on the threshold. 'We've already done away with enough traditions to bother with any more, don't you think?'

He shrugged, leaning down to brush his lips over hers. 'I don't indulge because it's tradition. I do it because I want to.'

Unable to help herself, she reached up and framed one taut cheek in her hand. 'What else do you intend to indulge in?' she asked saucily.

His smile was all red-blooded male arrogance. 'Patience, wife. You'll find out soon enough.'

Their laughter died, whittled away under the force of their lust as he set her down next to the immense emperor-sized bed.

Memories of their first time invaded her brain, plaguing her with doubts, making tremors surge from her toes upwards through her body. The first time she'd been a virgin. This time would be different. She'd given birth to his child and her body had changed. Both memorable events were enough to make her wonder...

'It'll be even better,' he murmured deeply, that uncanny ability of his to read her mind striking again. 'Because you're even more beautiful now than you were then. And you've borne my son.'

Tears stung the backs of her eyes and she rapidly blinked them away. If she knew nothing else, she knew Ekow loved his son—had already moved mountains for him. But Eva found she needed an untouchable place created for just herself. A moment in time she could call her own without the title of *mother* overshadowing it.

'But I take you as my wife. When I'm deep inside you, it'll be because I desire you as badly tonight as I did the first time we met.'

His intuition was eerily uncanny, and she would've been a little bit frightened had he not reached for the ties that secured her dress. With one firm tug the dress fell open, displaying the lace and satin lingerie set that formed part of her wedding trousseau.

Eva hadn't expected the evening to end this way when she'd put it on a little over three hours ago. But she was fiercely glad she had when his expression altered, a stamp of desire deepening in his face as his gaze scoured her.

'Every inch of you, every curve, is exquisite,' he breathed, his nostrils flaring as he leaned in close and inhaled her scent. 'I can't wait to be inside you.'

His words had the desired effect.

She swayed towards him, uncaring about being too eager. She couldn't stop. Ekow Quayson possessed the ability to tap into her deepest sexual desires, effortlessly stoking the flames until she feared she would lose her mind.

'Please… Kiss me.'

'All in good time, wife,' he growled.

He took his time to slide her sleeves down her shoulders and arms, inciting tiny fireworks with each glide. By the time the material pooled at her feet Eva could barely stand.

Large hands grasped her waist, easily spanning it.

In the next moment he'd yanked her close, plastering her almost naked body to his clothed one.

Bypassing her mouth, he trailed his lips down the side of her neck, gliding his tongue over her fluttering pulse, down her collarbone to the valley between her breasts, still cupped by her bra.

His kisses trailed over her skin, making her breasts go heavy and the peaks diamond-hard. Between kisses he murmured words of praise, drawing moans from deep in her throat as she fought to stay on her own two feet.

When he had done with torturing her, he straightened, his gaze burning into hers as he nudged her backwards onto the bed.

Eva propped herself up on her elbows, watched him step back and start to unbutton his shirt. She licked her lips, her hunger threatening to completely overwhelm her.

When her thighs twitched, he smiled. But it was a strained smile, the evidence of his own arousal framed thickly behind his fly.

Shirt discarded, he trailed his gaze feverishly over her body as he unbuttoned his trousers and slowly eased his zip over his erection.

At his unguarded flinch, she felt more dampness pool at her core, the blatant evidence of his state turning her on.

'You like that?' he asked in response to her helpless moan. 'You enjoy seeing your effect on me?'

'Yes,' she replied, unable to act coy. He did that to her, this man.

Moments later he was gloriously naked, coming

closer, prowling over her on the bed. Staring deep into her eyes, he slid one hand behind her back and effortlessly snapped open her bra.

His nostrils flared as her breasts spilled free. His thick groan was music to her ears. And then all sense of time and place disappeared as he dropped his head and captured one nipple between his lips.

Arching her back, Eva silently pleaded for more. He delivered. His hands, lips, teeth and tongue pleasuring her in ways she'd imagined would remain only fevered memories shaped by their first time together.

By the time he pulled her panties free she was hopelessly wet, aching and needy, ready to plead for mercy.

No plea was needed, because Ekow was equally driven, hunger stamped in his every movement as he reached for the foil packet inside the bedside drawer.

With far too sexy movements, he sheathed himself. Then dropping back off the bed, he stood at the side. Gloriously male, unashamedly aroused, he grasped her behind the knees and firmly parted her.

At the sight of her damp core, he groaned again, his breath escaping in harsh pants has he tugged her body downwards. 'Watch me, wife. Watch me make you mine.'

The primitive throb in his words drove her further towards the edge. Barely able to hold herself up, Eva angled her gaze downward.

'Tell me to take you.'

'Please,' she whispered urgently. 'I need you.'

Satisfaction washed over his face. His grip tightened, the capable hands holding her still as he notched himself against her heated entrance. Then, with his gaze equally riveted on where they were almost joined, he thrust inside her with one slow, relentless drive.

Her long moan bled into his thick, utterly male grunt, and the outward sounds of their coming together quickened the lust between them.

With each thrust Eva felt her resistance eroding, the dreams and fantasies she'd forced herself to stop spinning unfurling, taking on a life of their own—one which involved the man who possessed her so completely. The only man capable of driving her to these frenzied heights where only bliss resided.

When his gaze shot up, commanding hers to his, she was helpless to resist. So, with their gazes locked on one another, her lips parted on a cry that went on for ever, his relentless pounding finally pushed her over the edge into unrivalled pleasure.

Eva was vaguely aware that she moaned his name, clutched his sweat-slicked shoulders a little too tightly, but she couldn't find the strength to ringfence the torrent of emotions he'd unleashed in her.

However, she took solace in his own undoing as he gave a rough shout of pleasure before his own release tumbled him over the edge.

For endless minutes she clung to him as their bodies cooled and their breaths steadied. When self-awareness began to creep in she tried to hold it at bay, to revel in this moment for a few seconds longer. Only for it to be compounded when she gave a helpless protest as he pulled out of her, leaving her empty.

Watching him walk away towards the bathroom didn't alleviate the bereft feeling inside her. Unbidden, her gaze drifted towards the pillows. Then to the clothes on the floor.

They'd been in such a rush that they hadn't discussed what happened after this. Did she return to her bed? Did she want to?

No on both accounts, her heart screamed. But then wasn't it her heart she was risking by staying?

'You're staying right here,' Ekow's deep voice said from the bathroom doorway. His eyes dared her to countermand his command.

She'd grown far too vulnerable, far too raw in the aftermath of lovemaking, and the sight of him returning, godlike, his eyes burning with the residue of passion, dissolved the last of her resistance.

Her breath caught as he dropped to his knees beside the bed. When he caught one ankle between his hands, she realised that they'd made love without taking off her shoes. For some absurd reason, that drew laughter from her throat.

His gaze dashed up to meet hers, a ghost of a smile quirking his lips. 'Is this an interesting preference I should note?' he asked.

She shrugged. 'I wouldn't know. I've only ever been with you, so I guess we'll have to find out together.'

He stiffened, his eyes widening, locking on hers. 'What did you say?' he rasped, his voice raw and uneven.

Eva straightened, attempting to pull her heel out of his grasp, but he held on. 'You heard me.'

His stark astonishment would've made her laugh if she hadn't sensed his mounting tension.

'You were a virgin the first time we had sex?'

She squirmed beneath the fierceness of his gaze. 'Yes, I was. And before you give me a speech about not telling you, it was my choice.'

A flash of displeasure rushed over his face before he exhaled loudly. 'Nevertheless, I wish I had known.'

She tilted her head. 'Why? What would you have done differently?'

The question seemed to take him by surprise. 'I don't know,' he replied. 'Virgins are not my thing. Not until you, apparently.'

She told herself not to feel in any way special, but her heart refused to listen. It attempted to sing as he rose, discarded her shoes, and placed her in the middle of the bed.

Sliding in beside her, he pulled her close.

Utterly unable to help herself, Eva curled a hand on his chest, pillowed her cheek on one shoulder and let a little bit of that dream seep in.

She'd been a virgin.

He hadn't even noticed.

A vein of disgust slid through him, cutting through the primitive satisfaction swelling in his chest.

As she moved against him, her eyelids beginning to drift shut, his brain scrambled to recall every detail of their first time together.

Had he been gentle? Or had he fallen on her like a ravenous monster? Dear God, had he hurt her?

He remembered her pleasure, her eager hands reaching for him as they'd done tonight, her nails digging into his back.

Her sweet, insane snugness.

He wanted to be satisfied that he'd pleased her enough to take away the discomfort of her first time, but a frown slowly crept across his face as he replayed her words.

Why had she kept it a secret? Had she been afraid it would alter the way he felt about her? How *did* he feel about her?

His frown deepened, spikes of apprehension running alongside the primitive possessiveness.

So many emotions.

He silently shook his head. How very effortlessly she seemed to trigger them. Trigger *him*. And he'd asked for all of it.

He'd discovered a new emotion—the tireless love a father could have for his son—and now he was eager to experience more. When all he'd ever seen before were the extremes of love.

His brother Fiifi had been violently in love with Amelie's sister, while his father had channelled what little he'd felt towards one son, to the complete abandonment of the other two.

Ekow had vowed never to be like his father, but what safeguards did he have in place to avoid turning out like his brother? Especially if he let all these messy emotions in?

Sex for the sake of it, he decided grimly. It had never failed in the past. Why would it fail him now?

It wouldn't, he concluded. The wild possessiveness he'd felt for Evangeline just now was because he'd been her first. It would pass.

As would this insane rush that flowed between them

every time they so much as looked at each other. In the end all that would remain was sex for the sake of it.

And their son.

He was fine with that.

And he'd repeat that to himself until he believed it.

CHAPTER TEN

CAPE VERDE. As magical as Paris.

Eva hadn't been at all surprised to discover that Ekow owned a sprawling villa on the northernmost point of the island.

Over the past two weeks she'd discovered a lot about her husband.

He despised mushrooms. He spoke fluent Portuguese, alongside a handful of other languages—a talent she'd discovered she enjoyed when he used it in the bedroom.

Best of all, he made love as if was born to do it.

Eva was mildly stunned that she hadn't lost her vocal cords by now, with the amount of screaming she'd done during their honeymoon.

It was almost as if he wanted to prove something to her—to show her that, now she'd agreed to it, when they made love each lovemaking would be more mind-blowing than the last. To show her that beyond their son they had new common ground.

But the growing well of disquiet that had plagued these past few days was growing as the days ticked down to their return to Accra. Because with every moment spent in his presence she felt her foundations crumbling. Felt the reasons why this couldn't be a real marriage being eroded. The thought that she might be left vulnerable piled dismay on the anxiety. Because nothing had changed besides adding mind-blowing sex into the equation. Every scrap of love Ekow possessed was reserved for Leo—his reason for marrying her. While she feared she was in danger of being unable to contain her emotions to just Leo.

The growing alarm, and the need to stop herself from making the foolish mistake of falling for her husband, made her track him down to his study. The door was ajar. She paused in the doorway, her breath catching as she watched him finish a call.

His gaze found hers before travelling the length of her body, heating up with each second.

When the call ended he sprawled back in his seat, his eyes still fixed on her in a blatant declaration that said sex wasn't far from his mind. 'Is there something I can help you with, Eva?' he drawled.

She entered and shut the door behind her, clearing her throat to dissipate the sex-drenched atmosphere. 'Yes. It's about Quayson House. I feel as if I'm in a fishbowl there.'

One eyebrow slowly lifted, a brooding look entering his eyes. 'Hardly.'

'I know it's a mansion and all that. But you grew up there. You're fine with endless streams of staff running around and people visiting each other at the drop of a hat. You're used to it. I'm not. Put yourself in my shoes for a moment.'

'So you want to move?'

She sucked in a deep breath. 'Yes.'

'Are you planning to take me for half of what I own too, or going the whole hog and claiming everything while you're at it?'

There was amusement in his tone, but there was the bite of something else too.

She lifted her chin, feeling pride and hurt like twin arrows, seeking a bullseye within her. 'Neither. You can rest easy. You have nothing that I want.'

He regarded her steadily, his gaze growing more mocking by the second. 'Really? Nothing at all?'

Heat filled her face, and the memory of screaming his name and begging for more of his searing brand of possession ricocheted through her mind. 'You know what I mean.'

His face tightened. 'Perhaps. But for the sake of clarity you should spell it out.'

She took a deep breath that didn't quite reach her lungs because of the curious snag of pain beneath her ribcage. 'The house in Aburi. I'd like to live there full-time with Leo.'

His face tightened. 'Somehow we seem to find ourselves back to debating separate residences. Anyone would think you can't stand the sight of your husband. But we both know that's not quite true, is it?'

'Yes... No... Can we stay on point, please?'

He gave an eloquent shrug, drawing her much too avid gaze to the sleek symmetry of his body. 'That's the great thing about multitasking, sweet wife. We can discuss the subject of you attempting to live under a separate roof *and* sex. All at once. Would you like me to prove to you how eager you are for the latter beneath all that bluster?'

For embarrassingly long seconds she was stymied by the need to say *yes*. To kick the vital subject of moving residence and common sense to the kerb, stride over and slide into his lap.

She'd run her hand over the designer stubble that called to her fingers, cup his nape and drag his mouth to meet hers. She'd savour those velvety lips for moan-making minutes before letting her tongue tangle with his…

A slow-motion replay of doing just that held her mind motionless for a handful of seconds. Only the slow, smug smile sliding across his lips roused her from her erotic musings.

'The only subject I wish to discuss right now is the Aburi house and my moving into it.'

For an age, he stared at her. Then he nodded. 'If that is what you want.'

Before she could take a breath that was puzzlingly wrapped in disappointment, he added, 'But you won't be living there on your own. I take your point that Quayson House place might be overwhelming for you, but where my wife and son go, I go. No negotiation.'

When disappointment immediately turned into an illicit thrill at his words Eva knew she was in trouble. 'Okay…thanks.'

She turned to leave.

'Angel?'

She curbed the punch of pleasure that hit her some-where in the chest at the nickname.

'Why do you call me that?' she demanded. Exasperation erupted out of her, because she was genuinely alarmed by how much she loved his special abbreviation of her name.

'Because it suits you. I'm not naive enough to think angels are benign beings. You project being a peacemaker and nurturer when it suits you. But I also know you have claws you're not afraid to show when you feel the need to.'

Foolishly intrigued, she retraced her steps. 'And you like that?'

An entirely too arrogant smile crossed his sensual lips, drawing her attention to the delicious curve, reminding her how desperate she'd been to taste them last night.

'Have I not shown you yet how much? Perhaps you need a refresher?'

That she considered his raspy invitation for more than a fraction of a second told her how far gone she was. He watched her gaze flicker over the furniture in his office, his smile growing more smug as her breath caught. As images tumbled through her mind that drew her nipples into sharp points and made her panties damp.

God, she really needed to get herself under control around him. But why the urgency? Why not enjoy the sensuality he'd repeatedly promised and had more than delivered?

Where was the harm?

The question triggered a kernel of self-preservation she needed to hang onto. A warning that she risked more than falling prey to sexual decadence.

That she risked her heart.

His smile started to dim, and a displeased circumspection entered his eyes. 'I see the overthinking is starting again…'

'Someone has to do it. Did you want to talk to me about something else?'

'Yes. One of your clients.'

Her eyes widened at the name he tossed out. 'What about them?'

'They're a subsidiary of a business I own.'

Her heart caught for a different reason. 'So?'

'So I've been vetting your work. And I've made a decision about it.'

She settled her hands on her hips. 'You couldn't interview me, like anyone else? And what do you mean, you've made a decision?'

He took in her stance, his lips quirking again. 'Would you have accepted a position offered by me without overthinking that too?'

'I guess now we'll never know.' She turned to walk out, a larger kernel of hurt lodged in her midriff.

'Evangeline.' The firm bite of her name made her pause. 'I reached out to your previous employer.' When she froze, he shook his head. 'No, not the one you decorated with your drink the night we met. The director of that company, who was disappointed to see you go. He spoke of your work in glowing terms. So has everyone else you've worked for on a freelance basis since.'

She glanced over her shoulder. 'I know the quality of my work.'

'Then you won't think I'm practising nepotism when I offer you a position. And neither will anyone else.'

'Do you really care what anyone thinks?'

He gave a supremely arrogant shrug. 'Not especially. But I know you do.'

Why did that snag at something vital inside her? Why did it threaten to melt all the hardened edges she needed to keep around him? She should be annoyed he'd gone behind her back, but instead she felt…oddly treasured… What did that say about her?

He pushed a file towards her and she brushed the question away, a little too eager to sidestep it.

'What is this?' she asked.

He nudged his square chin at her. 'Take a look. Let me know if anything in there interests you.'

The list of his business interests was jaw-dropping. And within each one were positions that made the professional in her silently moan in envy. If she hadn't quit her job she'd be in one of these positions by now.

But then if she hadn't quit her job she wouldn't have walked into the Quayson Hotel bar. Wouldn't have met Ekow Quayson. Wouldn't have had her son…

She glanced up to find his far too perceptive eyes fixed on her. She lowered her gaze again, before he could read the direction of her thoughts.

Not all the positions were available, of course. But there were enough to tempt her. Especially the one at the Accra headquarters of Quayson Bank.

Again she stifled the voice questioning her true motive behind considering that particular position. So what if Ekow worked in the same building? They'd probably hardly ever see each other…

'The suspense is killing me,' he murmured. 'Would you like me to choose for you?'

'I'm completely capable, thank you.'

His mouth twitched but he said nothing. Merely sprawled back in his chair, a mogul completely at home in his billion-dollar playground.

Her gaze zeroed in on the position where her husband would be close by. Impatient with analysing why she should refuse something she wanted, she closed the file. 'I'd like to interview for the senior accountant position in the PR department at the bank.'

The gleam deepening in his eyes indicated that she'd chosen as he'd expected. Perhaps as he'd intended.

Enough.

'Done. But I want something in return.'

'What?'

'Lunch with me when we're both in the building. Every day.'

It was the last thing she'd expected him to say, and something far too excitable tugged inside her. *Again.* 'I… Why?'

His gaze raked over her in a slow, leisurely perusal that left her even more breathless. 'Do I need a reason to have lunch with my wife?'

'I… No, but…'

He raised an eyebrow. 'But?'

She pressed her lips together, alarm rising once more as she felt the erosion of her resistance and disregarded it anyway. 'Fine. If I'm not busy.'

He rose slowly to his feet, his large body completely absorbing every frame of her attention. She'd seen him in different forms of clothing, but Ekow in a formal suit would always remind her of those electric moments when she'd first set eyes on him. Those hours, then days of madness, when she'd experienced true sexual awakening for the first time.

She stayed in place as he rounded his desk and sauntered towards her. 'You want me to earn your attention? Is that it? I could push for marital privilege...' he taunted, with a smile still playing at his lips.

When he smiled like that she wanted to tell him he could push for anything he wanted. She stemmed the careless response just in time. 'You could... I wouldn't recommend it, though. Do I need to remind you of the last boss who attempted to push me?'

'No—and I would never be that offensive.'

'Good.'

She'd expected a flat refusal to the living in Aburi proposal. An argument at the least. His agreement to that and his offer of a job had shocked her.

Accomplishing his agreement to one and being surprised with the other drew a smile from her as she looked up at him.

He raised an eyebrow. 'I take it you're pleased with the outcome of your visit?'

She affected a careless shrug. 'Maybe.'

He moved closer, and her heartbeat escalated, her skin heating up. 'Something else you want to fight about, wife?'

Another thing she'd learned during their honeymoon was that Ekow loved a challenge. Enjoyed it when she stood up to him. She'd never have believed it of herself, but she had discovered a kinky side to their lovemaking she was growing alarmingly addicted to.

'Maybe you should leave a few items of clothing on the floor, or insist I put on sun cream a hundred times a day like you did yesterday. See how that works out for you.'

He gave a low, husky laugh as he closed the distance between them. Her breathing went haywire.

'I could do that…or I could go straight to the thing I most enjoy about you.'

She stepped back as he towered over her—not because she was afraid of him, but because she knew he would follow. True enough, he mock-prowled after her across his study, then pinned her against a perfect space between two tall bookshelves.

Eva could barely breathe past the anticipation and hunger spiralling through her. He reached for the tie that secured her midriff-baring top, tugging it open to reveal the bikini she wore underneath.

'Leo—'

'Is asleep—or you would've brought him with you. Besides, I heard you singing him to sleep via the monitor.' He jerked his head over his shoulder. 'So nice try.'

'I do my best,' she replied tartly, unable to stop the smile curving her lips.

His gaze raked over her face, his own amusement disappearing. 'You're beautiful,' he rasped thickly.

His words literally made her sag at the knees, and she was thankful she was propped up against the wall. When he reached for the button to her tiny denim shorts she let the last of her resistance fall away.

She was naked within seconds.

For the sake of equality, she reached for his clothes, her eager hands sending more than one button flying off his shirt as she dragged it down his tightly muscled biceps.

Their fever continued to grow, until at last he surged inside her, his grunt of pure male satisfaction melding with her cries, her body opening up to his complete possession.

Another thing she'd discovered about her husband was his seemingly endless stamina. Repeatedly he sent her to the edge, only to withdraw, letting her hunger build and build, before cupping her breast, squeezing her nipples between thumb and forefinger and growling in her ear, 'Come for me, Angel.'

As if responding to a Pavlovian trigger, her climax hit her with full force, bliss washing over her until she was gladly drowning, her body screaming with pleasure as her husband possessed her.

He barely gave her time to catch her breath before he was spinning her around, pushing her chest into the wall and thrusting inside her from behind.

'Sweet heaven, I can't get enough of you,' he growled.

Those echoes of bewilderment in his voice had grown increasingly stronger in the past few days—just as hers had built since that night in Paris. Eva knew they were teetering on a dangerous edge. Or perhaps she had already tipped over. She'd refused to listen to the alarm bells growing steadily louder, and she knew her heart was involved somewhere in there.

How could it not be?

From their first meeting she'd known those hours spent with Ekow were too good to be true. The distance she'd created this time, with their agreement, was the buffer she'd needed not to lose her heart.

But then Paris had happened.

Just like their nights together the first time, she'd let

herself be drawn deeper, allowed the fantasy to linger a little longer. Soon the chemistry would fade, she knew. Ekow would go back to his life, and she would be left with the same craving she'd endured before the reality of her pregnancy had shifted her focus.

Only this time it would be ten times worse. Because she'd have to endure living under the same roof as Ekow, being confronted with the very thing she couldn't have.

'Angel?'

Her heart lurched, that name on his lips creating its own set of problems. 'Eva,' she insisted.

Against her neck, she felt him smile. 'Angel,' he repeated.

She shook her head, blind panic swirling inside her. 'I have to go.'

'Where's the fire?' he murmured as his lips continued to wreak havoc on her senses.

'Give us time… I'm sure we'll find it.'

When she glanced over her shoulder she saw a faint frown had creased his eyebrows. Knowing he was about to demand an explanation, she hurriedly tugged on her shorts and top.

'Um…thank you for agreeing to the Aburi thing. And for the job offer.'

He continued to watch her with those piercing eyes as he pulled his own clothes back on.

Afraid he would see through her to the heart of her fears, she hurried out of the door.

In the shower, minutes later, she braced her hands on the wall, a multitude of questions cascading over her. When she couldn't find an answer to a single one, Eva

knew that what awaited her was a devastation the likes
of which she'd never known.

She objected to him calling her Angel only because
each time he murmured the name in bed, or tossed it
out casually across the breakfast table, she feared she
was falling in love with her husband.

Perhaps she already had.

Her husband who had only married her to secure
his son.

He'd given her no promises other than sex. He'd delivered on that promise in the last two weeks. *And nothing else.*

Her heart squeezed as she faced the hard truth. She'd
been too hasty in getting excited about Ekow wanting
to live with her and Leo. Surely he would grow bored
with living in Aburi after a few months. And then what?

They were married now. There was no escaping him.
But she could keep him at arm's length. Take steps to
avoid further devastation before it completely annihi-
lated her.

She turned off the shower, the decision weighing
heavily on her heart. By the time she was dressed again
she'd accepted it was the only solution.

She had to resist her husband at all costs—before
she fell deeper into the hell that was loving a man who
didn't love her back.

Something had changed.

One minute his wife had been crying out in ecstasy
in his arms, and the next she'd been freezing him out.

At least she hadn't given him the clichéd excuse of
having a headache when he'd tried to pull her into his

arms in bed last night. She'd simply speared him with those chocolate-brown eyes and shaken her head. 'Not tonight.'

Call him arrogant, but Ekow knew it wasn't because she'd suddenly developed an aversion to him. He'd seen the desire lurking in the backs of her eyes, read the familiar signs of arousal in her body.

But he'd accepted her rejection, nonetheless.

Then he'd lain there for the rest of the night with panic growing in his gut.

Something was wrong. Something had happened after that searing sex against the wall. Had he been too rough on her? Too demanding?

He frowned.

The woman he'd come to know in the last six weeks wouldn't have hesitated to put him straight had he stepped out of line. She'd been right there for an intensely satisfying ride. Right until the very end, when she hadn't been able to get away fast enough.

His gaze flicked to the bedroom door on his private jet, as it had done repeatedly since they'd taken off from Cape Verde three hours ago. He wanted to storm in, demand to know what was going on. But she had the buffer of their son between them, and the last thing he wanted was to disturb Leo's sleep.

There would be time enough, he reassured himself, settling back to work he could barely concentrate on. The past few weeks had shown him he'd been right to take this path. They were compatible in so many areas of their lives.

So what if love wasn't involved?

That dip in his chest occurred again, mocking the statement, urging him to re-examine his belief.

He shook his head, denying it. Sex was all it was.

Sex and all the other things that made him think about her when she wasn't in his presence...crave her even more when she was.

His frown intensified.

That description skated far too close to what Fiifi had said he'd felt with Amelie's sister, Esi. What Atu had described to him one drunken night when he'd been parted from his wife—a rare occurrence that had seen his brother track Ekow down to help alleviate the pur-portedly agonising feeling of missing his wife.

Ekow had scoffed then. He wasn't scoffing now.

What did that mean?

He jerked to his feet, striding in the opposite direc-tion to the cockpit.

Five minutes later he sensed he was irritating his pilots with his relentless questions and retreated back to his work.

He *wasn't* developing feelings for his wife. He sure as hell wouldn't let himself stray to either extreme side of emotional spectrum that had plagued his father and his brother—rejection or obsession.

He simply wouldn't allow it.

He was simply experiencing the adverse effects of being far too long absent from his desk. A return home to normality would put everything back in its proper place.

CHAPTER ELEVEN

THE DAYS FOLLOWING their return home cemented Eva's conviction that moving to Aburi was her only option.

Her mother-in-law's cool reception of her had turn into frost.

It would all have been so much of a cliché had she not been living it.

Even more alarmingly, Ekow hadn't put up a fight when she'd chosen to stay in her own suite on the night of their return and the following nights.

Yes, she'd intended to keep him at arm's length. But was it already over?

Her heart squeezed, adamantly opposed to her rare reluctance to fight this particular battle. What was the point of fighting when she knew she'd lose?

A week after their return, she entered the living room after putting Leo to bed for his afternoon nap, to find her mother-in-law waiting there for her.

'Ekow tells me you're moving to the Aburi villa.'

Her heart clenched. 'Yes,' she replied.

Naana Quayson's eyes narrowed. 'Why?'

'I don't think that's any of your business,' she retorted briskly.

Her mother-in-law rose from where she had been seated, the Queen of the residence, wherever she invited herself. 'He's perfectly happy here. Why would you want to change that?'

'He may be—but I'm not.'

'Marriage is not about just doing what you want, young lady. Marriage is about accommodating your husband's every need.'

Alarm, heartache and fear bubbled up inside her and she slowly balled her hands and shoved them into the pockets of her sundress. 'And I thought marriage was about compromising, doing everything in your power to make *each other* happy—not just one party.'

The older woman's face tightened. 'Be careful—'

'Of what?' She tipped up her chin in defiance. 'I seem to be getting warnings every time I turn around. I'm not forcing your son to do anything he doesn't want,' she said, but then felt a tug deep inside.

Had she pushed Ekow? Was that the reason for his withdrawal?

She shook her head.

It didn't matter now. She was leaving before she did the unthinkable and blurted out her love to a man who only wanted sex and a mother for his child.

'I'm sorry our decision is not to your liking. You're more than welcome to visit any time you want—with advance warning, of course.'

She turned on her heel, ignoring her mother-in-law's shocked face as she walked out. They hadn't discussed a date for their move to the mountains, but as she hurried down the hall Eva decided this was as good a day as any.

Locating the housekeeper, she instructed her to start packing her belongings.

Three hours later she was in another of those SUVs that seemed to miraculously cut through the heaviest of Accra traffic.

She was minutes away from the villa when her phone rang. Tentatively she answered.

'I'm informed that you're packed and heading for the mountains. Care to tell what the hurry is?' Ekow said, frost edging his voice.

'Care to tell me why it has to be later rather than now?'

He remained silent for several seconds. 'My mother is on her way to see me, I understand. Is there anything I need to know before she arrives?'

Eva let out a harsh laugh, startling her son. She reached out to soothe him as she answered. 'She's your mother. The privilege of dealing with her is yours.'

She hung up before he could reply, feeling a slash of shame for using the unpleasantness between his mother and her as a tool to put further distance between them.

But hadn't that distance been there all along? Temporarily cloaked with sex?

She shook her head in a wild bid to end her chaotic thoughts.

The truth was she was in love with Ekow.

The only thing that would stop the wrenching inside her chest was knowing it was reciprocated.

And it wasn't.

So she concentrated on Leo, shamelessly basking in his joyous existence. And as she let herself into the villa, as the memories of her last time there washed over her, she kept him close, pouring all the love she couldn't give his father into him.

In the following two weeks Ekow visited just once, to ensure that Leo was safely installed in his new home and healthy and happy.

And Eva resigned herself to the endless days of devastation that lay ahead of her.

He wasn't a coward.

But the evidence was irrefutable. Possibly marriage-ending.

Somewhere in his eagerness to secure his son and Evangeline to him, he'd abandoned the sixth sense he'd felt in Cape Town that Eva was hiding something from him.

Now, with his every breath he wanted to shoot the messenger—even if that messenger was his mother.

The chequebook stub from his parents' private account had been the fatal clue. His father hadn't bothered to hide his actions.

A cheque for one million dollars, written out to Evangeline Annan.

Ekow didn't doubt his father had been testing the woman who'd claimed to be carrying his child.

She'd failed. And she'd kept it from him.

He'd mentioned his father's habit of paying off 'nuisances' in Paris *and she'd said nothing.*

He wasn't a coward.

But he couldn't bring himself to storm up the mountain to confront her.

What could she say to redeem herself? Or, worse, what if she told him it had all been about money? Hadn't he bankrolled her brother to get him out of trouble and set him up on a path to success?

Sure, she'd left the Quayson Hills mansion, but with her new surname she could command the prestige and the power she'd claimed she didn't want anywhere in the world.

He hadn't demanded she sign a prenup. He wasn't perturbed at the thought that she might demand whatever she wanted from him. He had powerful lawyers to deal with that if need be.

But it was undeniable that the longer she stayed in the marriage the more clout she would have against him later. Perhaps she'd even attempt to take Leo from him.

He surged to his feet, striding to the window and back again as he'd done repeatedly since his mother had dropped the bombshell.

Had he read Eva so spectacularly wrong? The beautiful, laughing, vibrant woman who'd burrowed deep under his skin? Had those excuses he'd given himself about it all being about sex been so much hot air?

He wasn't a coward.

When he strode to his desk one last time and snatched up the phone to call his pilot, he told himself it was because of his son.

But even before he boarded the helicopter to fly to the mountains he knew it was because of *her.*

It had always been fundamentally because of her.

He'd gone to South Africa hoping he might see her again. He'd grabbed the chance to secure her to him in marriage the moment he'd discovered the existence of his son.

It had always been about her.

The used chequebook burned his chest as he alighted from the chopper twenty minutes later.

She was waiting on the terrace, a vision in white, her beauty so devastatingly breathtaking he felt something shake inside him, triggering a searing hunger which confirmed once and for all that what he felt for this woman was more, *much more* than he'd ever anticipated.

She raised her chin as he drew closer, those arms wrapped around herself in fierce defence. 'I didn't know you were coming.'

'Do I need an invitation to visit my own home?'

Her lips pressed together, and it was all he could do not to catch her in his arms and kiss those lips, demand a warmer welcome than the frostiness she was throwing at him.

'Where is Leo?'

Her eyes flashed at him. 'He's perfectly fine. He's had his evening bath and is playing in his crib. The nanny is with him.'

He nodded. 'We need to talk.'

Her eyes widened, and for a moment he fooled himself into thinking he saw alarm in there. The same alarm snaking through him at the thought of losing her, at the thought that there might not be a surmountable explanation for what she'd done. Because he wasn't sure he could stomach a wife who loved his money but rejected him… He'd had enough rejection to last him a lifetime.

When she nodded, he struck off down the hallway towards his study. He entered, held the door open for her, then shut it behind them before leaning against it, feeling a searing reluctance to start.

He was far too aware that this conversation might well fracture the fragile foundation of what he'd started building weeks ago.

Yes, at the time he'd loftily imagined sex was the answer to everything.

Her absence had shown him differently.

Shown him enough to stir up a grudging respect for what his brother had felt for Esi, because the no-holds-barred expression he'd in seen Fiifi's eyes the night he had passed away had held what Ekow was feeling now. Fiifi had even been hinting of giving up his place in the Quayson family and company for the woman he loved—a decision that would've caused much more chaos than had already existed in their families. *And he'd have done it because of love.*

'Are you going to talk, or just stand there brooding at me?'

He almost smiled because, even cornered, she was fearless. He straightened, reaching into his pocket as he strolled towards her. 'Would you care to explain this to me?'

Her gaze darted down, then flew back to his in wary alarm. His heart fell.

'Where…? How…?'

'I warned you not to keep secrets from me. I told you I would find out everything you were hiding from me eventually.'

Predictably, her chin notched higher, and she blasted him with a look so fierce he would've burned to a crisp were he a lesser man.

'What else can it be? This was your father's way of buying me off.'

'Which you accepted, of course?'

The faintest tremble seized her lips, before she clamped them together and steadied herself a moment. 'Of course. How else was I to remind myself of the sort of people I was dealing with?'

He frowned. 'What's that supposed to mean?'

'Your father offered me a million dollars to stay away from you—to pretend the child I was carrying wasn't yours. Everyone around you throws around money like confetti…like it'll solve every problem you have. I kept the cheque as a reminder on how *not* to bring up my son. *Your* son.'

An earthquake shook through him. 'You kept the cheque?'

'Did your spies not tell you what happened to the money?' she scoffed.

His jaw gritted. 'The cheque came from my parents' private account. I don't have access to the records. My mother showed this to me."

"Right. I guess now I know why she doesn't like me. And she thinks what, that I must've had some shady characters squirrel it away for when I need it?'

His eyes narrowed. 'It isn't beyond the realm of possibility, especially if you say you kept it.' The burning sensation was too much to contain. 'Dammit, Eva, I thought you were different. That you were above this!' He waved the infernal chequebook between them. 'I opened up to you in Paris. You know how I felt about what my father did. How I felt about his rejection.'

Her eyes were suspiciously wet, but they blazed all the same. 'Well, I thought *you* were different, too. But what have you given me to make me think so, hmm?

Fabulous sex? I reckon if I search hard enough I'll find someone else who will—'

A growl left his throat as he felt fear and jealousy congeal inside him. 'You'll have to rid yourself of me first. And I promise you that won't happen without a fight.'

Desolation settled on her face. 'Why? Why would you fight for me when you don't feel anything for me? You're ready to label me a gold-digger when all I was trying to do was stop you from feeling more pain.'

'What?'

'Yes, I could've told you about the cheque earlier. Maybe even in Cape Town. But when you told me your father had a habit of doing that, I thought you'd be devastated to know he'd done it with Leo, too. I just wanted to save you from being hurt further. But no. Everything I do has to contain an ulterior motive, doesn't it?'

The indictment shook through him, intensifying the quaking beneath his feet.

Dear God, he was going about this all wrong.

'You wanted to save me from pain?'

His voice wasn't as steady as he wished, and a terrible fear was taking hold inside him that the loss he'd feared was within seconds of being realised.

She rubbed a shaky hand over her temple. 'I find myself wanting nothing but the best for you. I risked rejection to tell you that you had a son because I believed you should know. I married you because—' She stopped, shook her head. 'More fool me, right?'

He jerked forward. 'No! Don't say that. You're not a fool. God, *I'm* the fool. I've missed what's important, Eva. What's right in front of me.'

'You don't really believe that. Staying away has been easy for you,' she accused, and he caught the trembling in her voice. 'You want to know what happened to the cheque? Stay here.'

Pivoting, she strode to the door and threw it open.

And, of course, because he couldn't stay there, couldn't let her out of his sight because he'd missed her so damn much, he trailed after her, his gaze eating her up as she launched herself up the stairs.

His heart leapt when she strode into his bedroom. Despite telling himself not to read anything into it, he couldn't shake the thought that she'd been sleeping in his bed, perhaps even clutching his pillows at night the way he'd been clinging to hers, pathetically attempting to catch her scent and alleviate the desperate loneliness and hunger inside.

He forced himself to concentrate as she strode out of the dressing room, a piece of paper clutched in her fingers.

'Here's your precious cheque. Take it and get out. I never want to see you again.'

His vision clouded. He fought through it. Took the cheque and tossed it over his shoulder, uncaring where it landed.

'No. Please. Let me make things right. I should've… I suspected you were keeping something from me, and normally I would have been relentless in finding out. But the feeling went away. Because here…' he pressed a hand to his heart '…where it counted, I knew whatever you'd done wasn't something I needed to fear. Forgive me. I… I don't want to lose you.'

'Lose what, exactly? What do you have besides our

son?' The agony in her voice tore at her. 'If I packed my bags right now and left, giving you equal rights to our son, would you even miss me?'

'Yes! It would kill me. Tell me what I need to do to make things right,' he pleaded again, holding his hands out to her. 'Please, Eva,' he croaked desperately.

He wasn't a coward. So he laid it all on the line. 'I can't breathe without you. Can't sleep…can't think.'

She laughed. 'And yet you made it so effortlessly easy for us to be apart.'

He frowned. 'Because I thought that was what you wanted.'

Her eyes widened. 'We agreed we would live here. Together.'

'And then you turned away from me. That day we made love in the study something happened, didn't it? Did I do something?'

She whirled away from him, but not before he spotted the sheen of tears in her eyes.

She shook her head. 'It doesn't matter now, does it? I'm a gold-digger who pocketed one million dollars—the mother of your child who you probably imagine is just hanging around for more.'

He stepped around her so he could see her face once again. Now the haze had cleared, he could see how devastatingly wrong he'd been. He just hoped it wasn't too late. 'You rejected a mega mansion in favour of a mountain villa out of sight of the great and the good of Accra. You could've deposited that cheque in your bank account within days of receiving it, but you didn't.'

'That proves nothing.'

He shrugged. 'It proves that what is happening between us isn't about money. I discovered this cheque existed a week ago, but I didn't do anything about it because, again, it wasn't about money. It was about fear. I didn't want to risk you telling me that you wanted to live here on your own. Without me. I couldn't stand the thought of that. I can't stand the thought of being away from you, Eva.'

Slowly she turned around. 'Why? You still haven't given me a good enough reason, Ekow.'

Emotion shook through him and for the first time he welcomed it—good or ill. Because he would walk through flames for this woman. Rip his own heart out if it would make hers beat. For him. For Leo. *For them.*

'Because I love you. That evening at the bar you took my breath away, and you have been taking my breath away ever since.'

He saw her tremble and could barely stop himself from reaching out for her. He stood still, watching her eyes widen with disbelief. And hope?

'You love me?'

'So much. I fooled myself into thinking it was just sex. I invited you to stay with me that weekend because I thought I could work you out of my system. When I woke to find you gone I felt empty. More empty than I had a right to feel after just two nights. But you've never strayed from my mind. The moment I discovered my hacker was in Cape Town I had to be on the plane. Even when I didn't know how to find you, just to be in the same city as you stopped the aching inside. And when you opened the door to me there was no way I could let you get away. I love our son, and I thank the heavens every day for his existence—and not just because he brought me back to you. But you have to know that I was always going to find you, Eva. It was only a matter of time. You're the missing piece I've been looking for all my life. I can live with you not loving me as much as I love you right now, but I can't live with the thought of a permanent separation. Please, Angel.'

He watched another tremor go through her, and inhaled sharply at the look that came over her face.

'That's what did it,' she murmured softly.

'What?'

'You calling me Angel that day in the study in Cape Verde.'

He shook his head. 'But I'd called you that many times before.'

Her arms dropped from their protective stance, and he felt the faintest shred of hope.

'I know. But something about the way you said my name that day scared me a little bit, because I knew I was falling in love with you.'

Hope surged wilder, filling his heart. 'You were?'

'Oh, yes. I've been falling in love with you since that first moment, Ekow. It was why I fled from you before dawn that weekend. I wanted to stay—so badly. But I didn't know how without risking my heart.'

His own heart turned over. With joy. With awe. With gratitude for the magnitude of the gift she was granting him.

'You will never have to risk your heart with me, my darling. I will treasure it. You have my promise. Always.'

Tears filled her eyes and he finally breached the gap between them, cupping her cheeks before swiping his thumbs beneath her eyelids, wiping away the drops that fell.

'I love you, Eva. I want you to remain my wife, please. Tell me what I need to do and I'll do it.'

'You're already doing it. You're right here, with me, giving me everything I've been yearning for. Please stay?'

'Of course I will. A thousand horses couldn't drag me away.' He paused then, grimacing before looking over his shoulder. 'Please forgive me for that,' he pleaded, nudging his chin at the cheque on the floor.

Without answering, she walked past him and picked up the cheque. Returning to him, she ripped it into a hundred pieces. 'I should've done this a long time ago.'

'Maybe. But maybe it was what we needed to push us into fighting for what our hearts desired.'

She swept back into his arms and he caught her up, his heart filling with true, pure love as he lowered his head and kissed her.

Several minutes later he lifted his head and grimaced at the tears filling her eyes all over again. 'I'd like my feisty wife back, please.'

She laughed. 'Don't worry, she's right here. But you need to give her a while to bask in this wonderful moment.'

He brushed his lips over hers again, sliding his arms around her waist to pull her even closer. 'Take all the time you need, my love. I'll be right here loving you, loving our son, through thick and thin.'

'Do you think your mother's going to start liking me now?' she joked.

His lips twisted. 'Don't worry. I will leave her in no

doubt that any further interference from her will not be welcomed. She will be told, firmly, that you are the woman for me. From now till eternity.'

Her lips trembled, and he kissed her once more simply because he couldn't not.

'I love you, Ekow,' she whispered.

That seismic phenomenon occurred again, and he knew he would experience the magnificent feeling repeatedly with this woman in his life.

'I'll do everything in my power to keep earning that love, Eva.'

'Angel,' she corrected softly. 'I like being your angel.'

'You are. For always,' he promised.

'Always…'

EPILOGUE

One year later

EVANGELINE STOOD NEAR the terrace railing outside her bedroom suite at their Aburi home, making sure to keep out of sight of the trio on the rolling lawn below.

Moments like these were little treasures she furiously hoarded and took out at the end of the day, when she counted her blessings.

Her lips curved in a smile, her heart leaping with joy as an almost-toddler's exuberant shrieks pierced the air, followed by unfettered giggles. Unable to help herself, she peered over the railing to see her son galloping across the grass on chubby legs, hotly pursued by two tall forms as he fled the threat of tickles.

'Are you shamelessly spying again?'

Her husband's low, deep and intensely sexy voice was followed a second later by his strong arms sliding over her hips to band low over her belly.

'I can't help it. It's all so…precious.'

Her voice thickened with emotion and Ekow's arms tightened reflexively for a moment before his head dropped into the crook of her neck.

'Hmm… And you do know Jonah will immediately stop if he catches you watching?' he murmured.

'It's uncool to let me see how much he adores his nephew, apparently,' Eva grumbled good-naturedly, relaxing back into her husband's chest.

In some ways the changes in her brother were nothing short of remarkable. His sullen moods had disappeared, and his enthusiasm for his studies and his outlook on the future were almost effervescent.

The last of Eva's misgivings had been laid to rest when she'd spoken to him in those weeks after he'd started at his new school, and they'd completely disappeared by his first visit home to Aburi. Watching him top his class consistently in the past year had been proud moments for them both.

But he was still a teenager, with strong views on how he needed to act—especially around his sister and the brother-in-law she knew he secretly hero-worshipped.

Hence her covert spying activities on the terrace.

'He's not the only reason you're in stealth mode, though, is it?' Ekow rasped.

Her heart somersaulted, and her throat clogged all over again as her gaze drifted to the other figure trailing behind her brother and son.

The man's all-grey hair and slightly stooped form spoke of his advancing age. When he turned slightly and she caught the indulgent smile he beamed at her son love surged through her anew.

She didn't need to hear his voice to recall the strong Dutch accent. To see shades of him in Leo's face when he laughed.

Henry Rodling.

Her father.

Eva experienced another *pinch me* moment when, sensing her scrutiny, the older man looked up and raised a hand in greeting. Her own hand shook a little as she returned his wave, an overwhelming sense of blessing and gratitude washing over her at the knowledge that while she'd been wishing for him, her father had been yearning for the child her mother had forbidden him from ever knowing after their brief relationship had soured.

Like Leo's had been for her, Eva's conception had come as a surprise to her mother. And to Henry when she'd eventually informed him. Her father, a low-income earning businessman living in Amsterdam, already supporting a large family consisting of his elderly parents and three siblings, hadn't been in any position to support a newborn—a fact which her mother hadn't taken very well and so had forbidden him from ever contacting her again.

Henry had felt as if he'd had no choice but to accept her mother's wishes to stay away. But he had always meant to find Eva, and had been attempting to do exactly that for the last five years with no success—until Ekow's stellar investigators had located him. Knowing that had helped her heal the wounds of abandonment a little quicker, leaving only budding love and the hope of a deeper relationship in future.

'I don't know how I'm ever going to thank you for finding him,' she said to the man who was the reason for her unfettered happiness, her reason for breathing. The love of her heart, mind and soul.

'You don't ever need to thank me for making your happiness my priority. Finding your father is a fraction of what I should give you in return for the treasure you've given me in yourself, our son and Jonah. In the love I never believed I'd find that you bless me with every second of every day.'

Unable to speak for a moment, she reached up and laid her hand against his cheek, glorying in the taut, warm skin beneath her touch and the kiss he trailed over her palm a moment later.

'But seeing as you're in a generous mood...' he drawled teasingly.

She started to laugh, then slapped her hand over her mouth before the sound travelled to the beloved family she was spying on. But, twisting her head, she let her eyes ask the question, making Ekow's own eyes gleam with sensual intent as he bent his lips to her ear once more.

'I'm very keen to make a withdrawal from the brownie points department...'

Pivoting in his arms, she slid hers around his neck. 'I really didn't think it through before granting you unlimited access, did I?'

He shrugged. 'With the type of interest rates you earn with that deal, you'll never experience a negative return.'

His shameless wink drew more laughter. 'Can we dispense with the banking lingo now, please?'

He sighed. 'And here I was on a roll. But if you're keen to move on, let me interest you in something else...'

Before she could ask what, his head descended, its destination her very willing mouth.

He drew her further back from the railing and into

the bedroom as his tongue tangled with hers in a possessiveness that set her heart racing.

Within moments she was breathless, her body primed for the kind of exhilarating excitement only he could deliver. Still, she attempted to halt the dizzying rollercoaster by catching his hand when he tried to release the tie of the silk robe she'd thrown on after her mid-morning swim.

'Wait…we can't… Atu and his family will be here soon.'

'We can,' he countered heatedly against her throat. 'He texted to say they're running late. I texted back and told them to take their time. That means I have you to myself for a whole hour…at least. And I don't intend to waste another second. Now, tell me to show you how much I love you,' he growled thickly.

That tiny obstacle dispensed with, Evangeline sighed and melted into her husband's arms. 'Show me, my love. Please…'

Two hours later…

'Oh, my God, this *red red* is the best I've had in ages!'

Eva smiled indulgently at her sister-in-law, watching as she forked another bite of the addictive, sublime fried ripe plantain and black-eyed beans and smoked tuna stew into her mouth. 'You gush over every dish my housekeeper makes. I'm almost terrified you'll poach her one of these days.'

'Confession: she tried just before you arrived. Sadly for her, Ekow is Gettie's favourite,' Atu relayed in a deep, rumbling voice.

Amelie gasped, turning to glare at her husband. 'I can't believe you just snitched on me!'

'You'll forgive me, because you have a chef I know you'll kill to keep. And he makes amazing *red red*, too.'

Amelie sighed. 'Yes, Mensah is awesome, isn't he? I'll just have to convince Gettie to give me her recipe. It'll go down a treat at the resorts…'

The conversation moved from Gettie the housekeeper's magical talents to the Quayson Hotel Group and its upcoming exciting projects and Ekow tuned out, rising to fetch another bottle of wine from the cooler.

Bottle in hand, he paused, his gaze wandering over the family seated at the large banquet table they'd set out in the shaded terrace overlooking the gardens and swimming pool.

At one end of the table Henry was situated between Ekow's mother and Amelie's mother, and Ekow winced in sympathy at the not-so-low-key grilling the old man was undergoing.

Then his gaze drifted to Jonah.

The boy didn't know it, but Ekow intended to spend the rest of his life in gratitude that the prodigious teenager had hacked his bank and led him back to Evangeline.

A few other cousins, uncles and aunts had also invited themselves along for the Sunday meal, but he didn't mind. The more the merrier.

Then, as if drawn by sweet, compulsive magic, his gaze finally arrived on his wife.

Against the white halter neck dress her golden-brown skin glowed.

Yesu, she couldn't look more beautiful if she tried.

He didn't bother to calm his leaping heart. It existed solely for the woman who'd made him whole.

'Counting your blessings again?' Atu murmured from beside him, a trace of good-natured mockery in his voice.

Ekow dragged his gaze from Eva and met his older brother's. '*Our* blessings. Don't think I haven't seen that misty-eyed look you keep sliding to your own wife.'

His brother sighed. 'What can I say? I'm a hopeless sap when it comes to her.'

Ekow sniggered. 'Don't let the board members hear you say that.'

Atu shrugged. 'I'm still ruthless when I need to be, but Amelie has taught me that there's nothing wrong with opening your heart to the ones you love. The rewards are immeasurable.'

Ekow nodded, agreeing wholeheartedly. 'I wish Fiifi was here,' he confessed gruffly, after a moment of silence.

Atu swallowed, his eyes shadowing for a moment before he clasped Ekow's shoulder. 'He is, brother. And so is Esi. They wouldn't miss this for the world.'

A curious lump lodged in Ekow's throat as his gaze locked with Eva's. She hadn't heard their conversation, but the look in her eyes said that she knew his thoughts and his heart. That, like him, she was grateful they'd found the precious miracles they'd searched for their entire lives.

The missing pieces of their souls and a home founded in love.

* * * * *

Caught up in the drama of
A Vow to Claim His Hidden Son?

Then you're sure to fall for the first instalment in the
Ghana's Most Eligible Billionaires duet
Bound by Her Rival's Baby

Why not also check out these other
Maya Blake stories?

Kidnapped for His Royal Heir
The Sicilian's Banished Bride
The Commanding Italian's Challenge
The Greek's Hidden Vows
Reclaimed for His Royal Bed

Available now!

WE HOPE YOU ENJOYED
THIS BOOK FROM
HARLEQUIN
PRESENTS

Escape to exotic locations where passion knows no bounds.

Welcome to the glamorous lives of royals and billionaires, where passion knows no bounds. Be swept into a world of luxury, wealth and exotic locations.

8 NEW BOOKS AVAILABLE EVERY MONTH!

COMING NEXT MONTH FROM

HARLEQUIN

PRESENTS

#4017 A BABY TO TAME THE WOLFE
Passionately Ever After...
by Heidi Rice

Billionaire Jack Wolfe is ruthless, arrogant...yet so infuriatingly attractive that Katherine spends a scorching night with him! After their out-of-this-world encounter, she never expected his convenient proposal or her response, "I'm pregnant..."

#4018 STOLEN NIGHTS WITH THE KING
Passionately Ever After...
by Sharon Kendrick

King Corso's demand that innocent Rosie accompany him on an international royal tour can't be denied. Neither can their forbidden passion! They know it can only be temporary. But as time runs out, will their stolen nights be enough?

#4019 THE KISS SHE CLAIMED FROM THE GREEK
Passionately Ever After...
by Abby Green

One kiss. That's all innocent Sofie intends to steal from the gorgeous sleeping stranger. But her moment of complete irrationality wakes billionaire Achilles up! And awakens in her a longing she's never experienced...

#4020 A SCANDAL MADE AT MIDNIGHT
Passionately Ever After...
by Kate Hewitt

CEO Alessandro's brand needs an image overhaul and he's found the perfect influencer to court. Only, it's her plain older stepsister, Liane, whom he can't stop thinking about! Risking the scandal of a sizzling fling may be worth it for a taste of the fairy tale...

HPCNMRA0522

#4021 CINDERELLA IN THE BILLIONAIRE'S CASTLE
Passionately Ever After...
by Clare Connelly

Tormented by the guilt of his past, superrich recluse Thirio has deprived himself of the wild pleasures he once craved. Until Lucinda makes it past the imposing, steel-reinforced doors of his Alpine castle. And now he craves one forbidden night...with her!

#4022 THE PRINCESS HE MUST MARRY
Passionately Ever After...
by Jadesola James

Spare heir Prince Akil's plan is simple: conveniently wed Princess Tobi, gain his inheritance and escape the prison of his royal life. Then they'll go their separate ways. It's going well. Until he finds himself indisputably attracted to his innocent new bride!

#4023 UNDONE BY HER ULTRA-RICH BOSS
Passionately Ever After...
by Lucy King

Exhausted after readying Duarte's Portuguese vineyard for an event, high-end concierge Orla falls asleep between his luxurious sheets. He's clearly unimpressed—but also so ridiculously sexy that she knows the heat between them will be uncontainable...

#4024 HER SECRET ROYAL DILEMMA
Passionately Ever After...
by Chantelle Shaw

After Arielle saved Prince Eirik from drowning, their attraction was instant! Now Arielle faces the ultimate dilemma: indulge in their rare, irresistible connection, knowing her shocking past could taint his royal future...or walk away?

YOU CAN FIND MORE INFORMATION ON UPCOMING HARLEQUIN TITLES, FREE EXCERPTS AND MORE AT HARLEQUIN.COM.

HPCNMRB0522

"You cannot leave."

"Why not?"

"The storm will be here within minutes." As if nature
wanted to underscore his point, another bolt of lightning
split the sky in two; a crack of thunder followed. "You
won't make it down the mountain."

Lucinda's eyes slashed to the gates that led to the
castle, and beyond them, the narrow road that had brought
her here. Even in the sunshine of the morning, the drive
had been somewhat hair-raising. She didn't relish the
prospect of skiing her way back down to civilization.

She turned to look at him, but that was a mistake,
because his chest was at eye height, and she wanted to
stare and lose herself in the details she saw there, the
story behind his scar, the sculpted nature of his muscles.
Compelling was an understatement.

"So what do you suggest?" she asked carefully.

"There's only one option." The words were laced with displeasure. "You'll have to spend the night here."

"Spend the night," she repeated breathily. "Here. With you?"

"Not with me, no. But in my home, yes."

"I'm sure I'll be fine to drive."

"Will you?" Apparently, Thirio saw through her claim. "Then go ahead." He took a step backward, yet his eyes remained on her face, and for some reason, it almost felt to Lucinda as though he were touching her.

Rain began to fall, icy and hard. Lucinda shivered.

"I— You're right," she conceded after a beat. "Are you sure it's no trouble?"

"I didn't say that."

"Maybe the storm will clear quickly."

"Perhaps by morning."

"Perhaps?"

"Who knows."

The prospect of being marooned in this incredible castle with this man for any longer than one night loomed before her. Anticipation hummed in her veins.

Don't miss
Cinderella in the Billionaire's Castle,
available July 2022 wherever
Harlequin Presents books and ebooks are sold.

Harlequin.com

HPEXP0522